Alexander Russell

Voices of Doubt

Australian scenes and other poems

Alexander Russell

Voices of Doubt
Australian scenes and other poems

ISBN/EAN: 9783337313005

Printed in Europe, USA, Canada, Australia, Japan

Cover: Foto ©Andreas Hilbeck / pixelio.de

More available books at **www.hansebooks.com**

VOICES OF DOUBT:

AUSTRALIAN SCENES,

AND

OTHER POEMS

BY

ALEXANDER RUSSELL, B.D.

Vicar of St. Paul's Church, and Dean of Adelaide.

ADELAIDE: E. S. WIGG & SON

MELBOURNE: S. MULLEN

1884

ADELAIDE
ADVERTISER JOB PRINTING OFFICE,
OFF WAYMOUTH STREET.

PREFACE.

WORDSWORTH, speaking of his own time, said—

> . . . The world is too much with us:
> Getting and spending, we lay waste our powers. . . .

and his words must often be recalled in a community
where life is so largely occupied with things lying merely
on the surface of existence. There are few who do not
find themselves driven to seek times of retreat, wherein
the solemnities lying below the fair face of society are
those which absorb the thought. It was in obedience to
this impulse that most of the things in this volume had
their origin. "Sometimes," says Mr. F. W. H. Myers
(Modern Essays), "our relations to the Unseen will take
possession of the soul; thought is lost in love, and emotion
seems to find its natural outlet in spiritual aspiration
and prayer." In such moods it is no less natural that
meditative thought should seek articulate utterance in
some form of verse, in which subdued feeling in the very
act of expression is partly veiled. Beautiful scenes and
sacred characters in the life of long ago blend mysteriously
with the thoughts of the present.

In some of the scenes of Scripture much more is suggested than is actually said, and yet the more imaginative and sympathetic treatment of the narrative is hardly compatible with the conditions of prose interpretation. Some familiar stories, such as those of the Doubting Disciple, the Deaf Mute, the Widow's Son of Nain, and the Woman of Samaria, are here read, as it were, between the lines. Besides this, a considerable portion of the volume has a bearing, more or less direct, on the prevailing doubt of the age by which so many hearts have been saddened and depressed. But here again Mr. Myers has spoken some true words: "We know that the true controversy is no longer between those within and those without the walls of any given church, but on a wider scale and involving profounder issues. It is a controversy between Spiritualism and Materialism, between those who base their life on God and immortality, and those who deny or are indifferent to both." At the same time, a distinction is to be observed between intellectual error and that more deplorable unbelief which is of the moral nature. It has been a comfort to the present writer to think that the number of persons who act practically under the influence of a belief which they have not been able to formulate is greater than would be suspected by those whose only test of faith is adherence to a dogmatic standard; since between all who are following the guidance of an Inward Light there must be true unity of feeling. Among the active agents in the promotion of unbelief must also be reckoned the grotesque misrepresentations of Christianity in many popular discourses which leave in doubt either the equity or the omnipotence of Divine Love. Against all this it is needful that some protest should be made.

Two explanatory things respecting the present publication may be added. The study of the crime of Judas was completed in its present form before the author met with Mr. Hart's imaginative attempt to reproduce the personal history of the Betrayer, and, after reading it, he did not find any occasion to alter what he had written. As an afterthought, some pieces bearing on Australian scenery and life were interposed before the principal poem—if poem it can be called.

CONTENTS.

ERRATA.

On page 29, line 10, for " dialetic " read " dialectic."

On page 83, line 8, for " flung " read " thrown."

On page 108, line 21, for " grevious " read " grievous."

On page 153, after " Her empty pitcher " read

. . . . " as before "
" She oft had come. But to restore "

On page 197, line 20, for " bleeding heart " read " bleeding breast."

On page 248, line 16, for " his own " read " its own."

VOICES OF DOUBT AND OTHER POEMS

—◆·●·◆—

In Memoriam

F. D. M.

———

SEE him now, no better understood
   Than was his Master; in his kindling eye
The light was like a message from on high.
He was so noble, that ingratitude
But woke in him some tender pitying mood.
The crowd's vain babble passed him idly by,
A prophet he, " a voice," like John, "a cry "
That to the sad world in its orphanhood
Told of a Father.   In his brilliant youth
He sought, and not in vain, to feel his way
Through all the maze of thought.   In seer and sage
He saw but divers seekers, gone astray,
Yet catching glimpses of the central truth,
The Word Eternal witness, age by age.

Australian Sonnets.

I. ON THE BLUE MOUNTAINS N.S.W.

GOVETT'S LEAP.

WHAT earthquake shock, what lightnings in their play
    Brake up the valley in this sudden rift ?
The tools that Nature wields alone could lift
The rugged masses that we see to-day.
Perchance a deluge, sweeping on its way,
Through scaur and crag its awful channel cleft,
Confusedly bearing on its breast a drift
Of fragments here imbedded in the clay
That welded them together. Now once more
Earth's wounds are healed : the shaggy height
Wears its green mantle as it did before
The tempest smote it, and the lichens grey
Fleck here and there the cliffs, else black as night ;
So Nature smiles where raged the wildest fray.

II. ON THE SHORE.

THE wind is high, and, whitening o'er the main,
    The foaming billows hasten to the shore
Like beasts of prey half-glutted, that for more
Of death and ruin ravin still. The strain
Sung by the winds is like a moan of pain,
And Anger mutters in the sullen roar
With which the waters come : the strand is hoar
With foam. But still unto the depths in vain
The voice of terror in the rising gale
Makes its shrill cry—Storms reach not Ocean's heart:
There, there at last, tumultuous heavings cease.
So, though in hours of dread the cheek grows pale
When thunders roll and lightning flashes dart,
In life's great depths abides the soul of Peace.

III. ON THE PORT ELLIOT ROCKS, S.A.

HIGH up in safety on the granite cliff,
    I hear the sound that soundeth evermore
With vague uncertain meaning, on the shore.
Across the bay a tiny fishing-skiff

Shows visionary on the scene, as if
An airy white-winged spirit flitted o'er
Some mystic mere. The screaming sea-gulls soar,
Then dive for prey. Far off on land, the stiff
Gaunt trunks of trees like gloomy watchmen stand,
But the wild waters, raging at our feet,
Send far in air the blinding clouds of spray,
And ceaselessly on rock or yielding sand
Like frantic things with mad impatience beat:
So, age by age, the cliff is worn away.

Other Australian Sonnets will be found later in this volume.

Christmas Eve in Australia.

1.

I KNOW not Christmas in this guise:
　　A radiance as of summer time
　Turns night to day, and in this clime
The stars are gemlike in the skies.

2.

The Church roof shines like silver sheen:
　　A mantle that is not of snow
　On all things lies: the pale moon's glow
Casts strange enchantment on the scene.

3.

And yonder, Night upon her breast
　　The mystic cross her emblem wears,
　And through the laggard hours prepares
To hail the morn that Christ hath blest.

4.

Perhaps in such a night as this
　The shepherds in old Palestine
　Were watching, when the news divine
Came sweet with angel melodies.

5.

If what they saw they hardly wist,
　Although the atmosphere was rare,
　Yet might it happen even there
That o'er the spirit gathered mist.

6.

Long watching, to their drowsy eyes
　The angel-forms uncertain seemed :
　At first they were as men that dreamed
Who struggled with a great surprise.

7.

But as the flood of moonlight pours
　And leaves no nook unvisited,
　The joy that came to them has spread
And found its way to other shores.

8.

In northern lands, the winter's snow
　Is like a faint reflection cast
　Of Light that through the world hath passed,
As in the South, the moonlight's glow.

Christmas in the Adelaide Hospital.

1.

THEY make my bedside gay with flowers:
  They come to me with smiles, and fain
I think, would cheat me of my pain—
But oh, the weary, weary hours!

2.

I heard the waggons in the street
  All through the restless, livelong night:
  Before the earliest streak of light
I heard the busy footfall beat.

3.

They brushed away the dews of sleep:
  So eager for the coming day
  Did any think of us that lay
Through wakeful hours that slowly creep?

4.

And yet the night was not so lone:
  'Tis something when the dull time crawls
  To know that outside these bare walls
No sickly people make their moan.

5.

There came a breath upon my cheek,
  As if some helpful love were near,
  And now the voice itself I hear—
I hear the voice of kindness speak.

6.

The richer food I could not eat
  With which they celebrate their feast,
  But tender hands have brought, at least,
Some coolness to this fever'd heat.

7.

They soothe my sense, they bathe my brow,
  And from the gardens far away
  The wafted odours seem to say—
" For you our sweetest flow'rets grow."

8.

They minister, I think, to me
  As long ago they would have done
  To Christ Himself: in every one
Who suffers—Him they think they see.

9.

And so the thoughts of Christmas fill
  The saddest places, and the wine
  Of human love becomes divine—
Thank God, the Christ is with us still!

An Australian Easter Day.

NOW peaceful is the scene! A holy hush
  Has fallen on the landscape. On the hills
There mantles calm, and that clear depth of sky
Is like the smile of God, in harmony
With all of peace and blessing that the day
Breathes on us here. The leaves are hardly stirr'd :
Deep silence reigns like that within the soul
Whose clear-eyed faith rests calmly on the Christ.
This hush of softened feeling in the air
Is Nature's dumb response, as if the scene
That lives for ever in the view of Faith
Had laid its spell upon the breathing world.
Here for a moment happy eyes can see
This fair Creation reaching forth to us,
And thrilling with the holy Easter joy ;

For Nature is so quick and sensitive
To all that makes our life a solemn thing,
That in her changeful moods she answers back,
When clouds have darkened on the clear expanse
Of human thought, or now again its sky
Is clear.   Creation has its times of storm,
But soon they pass.   The wild wind dies away
As if some voice were saying—" *Peace, be still!*"
And then the calm that falls is more than spent
Exhausted rage of warring elements.
The Will that, on the Sea of Galilee,
Rebuked and stilled the voices of the storm,
Set laws to all things that they cannot pass,
And to the spirit's tumult whispers peace,
Although we hear no voice, and can discern
Uprising on the scene, no awful Form.
The world grows dearer to us when we see
That things familiar thus express to us
Some thought of love : the natural repose
Has links of close connection with the life
Of living men.   There is a soul of truth
In all things, and a Spirit speaks to us

With meaning which the soul can understand.

The life of man has many a Holy Week

In which the cruel Cross is almost more

Than mortal strength can bear: then all seems o'er.

The hope, the joy of life, lies crushed and dead,

Until there comes a resurrection morn,

When life begins to stir.   The Easter joy

Has echoes in a thousand human lives.

The former pangs were like discordant notes

To make the strain more sweet which sounds at last

When new capacities of feeling rise

From unimagined depths, and all the wealth

Of love within our nature is revealed.

The world of sense is full of parables

By which we read the meaning of our life.

The sleeper, smiling in his happy dreams,

Is one but lately overspent with toil,

And though he sleeps so well, the lines of care

Are seen too plainly with the rise and fall

Of breath.   There is a pathos in his sleep

To one who looks upon the languid limbs

And half obliterated signs of pain.

The story of a life is almost writ

Upon the weary overdriven man

Who, when at last the power to struggle failed,

Had nothing left but thus to cast himself

Into the lap of Slumber, laying there

The meek confession of his helplessness.

With that repose that now has come to him

The scene around him harmonises well ;

For Night bends over him, and holds her breath

Lest but the faintest murmur in the room

Should break the charm that holds his spirit bound.

So Tribulation leads the way to peace,

And as in sorrow there are mystic depths

We cannot fathom, and the pain itself

Pursued mysterious windings in the soul,

And passed all understanding, God's own love

Is like to it.   It cometh when the soul

Has ceased from all self-pity, and forborne

The urgent cry for help, content to wait

Till patience finishes her perfect work,

Not knowing love was speeding on the path.
But when the blessèd visitant has come,
It seems as if the faculty of joy
Had gather'd strength from things that strove with it.
When man has chasten'd all his earthly will,
The heart grows bountiful ; the springs
Of secret love break forth again and flow.
The world itself is changed, and Nature now
Waves her bright answer to his alter'd mood,
Smiling with eyes of utter peacefulness,
And all the world seems thrilling with the bliss
That pulsates in the renovated soul.
The thing that touches us is something more
Than speaks to sense : a chord of feeling thrills
Between the living spirit and the soul
Of Nature, and the very light of day
Is like a benediction.   The still air
Arrests its breathing, motionless with awe,
In presence of the peace that is of God.
No discord mars the harmony of life :
The past, the present, and the future blend
Their notes in music that is passing sweet.

All things are seen to have conspired in one
To make the ways of God more clear; and now
The present is suffused with thoughts of faith,
And Hope has risen on her pure white wing
To bear us onward in her airy flight.
Our sight is bounded : but a little way
Our thought can penetrate those azure depths.
But soon the veil will fall, and then the eyes
Whose poor horizon here so bounds the view
Will gain new insight when they see the whole.

1882.

The Epic of Hades.

IN that old world, though dim through mythic haze,
There move strange forms that, as they go and come,
Reveal the heart of ancient Heathendom,
And show us how there run through all the days
Prophetic thoughts. We see them kneeling raise
Their eyes to stony gods whose lips are dumb :
Some grovel sordid in the dust, and some
By deeds immortal move the world to praise.
Pure Innocence, opprest and held in thrall,
And heroes, glorious in celestial might,
Ambition, Hate, and stronger Love, are there.
The nobler spirits to the noble call,
And watchman voices, in the dead of night,
For dawn of morn the wistful world prepare.

Voices of Doubt.

"*THE twilight of the world was prone*
" *To faiths or fancies of the brain,*
" *And men of doubting mind were fain*
" *To hide the thoughts they dared not own:*
" *The world was eager for belief,*
" *And they, suspected by the good,*
" *Misconstrued, never understood,*
" *Consumed their heart in secret grief,*
Said one pale student, eager-eyed,
Who took this cursory review,
" *But it is better to be true*
" *Than merely on the winning side.*

The times are changed, and doubters now
Go forth amid the crowd to preach
With little reticence of speech,

Yet with a shadow on their brow,
As if a bright triumphal air
Were cross'd by some pathetic strain,
And there are wailings as of pain
Beneath their gospel of despair.
They see dissolving in a mist
Which Fancy touches with its gold,
The substance of the tale oft-told
Of this or that evangelist:
And yet the voice grows tremulous,
And soften'd feeling intervenes,
When in the tender Gospel scenes
The soul of nature speaks to us.
As when a picture of the lost
Brings back the time that once was dear,
The past is sounding in their ear,
And haunts them almost like a ghost.
And yet, to echo with the crowd
The phrases of a creed worn out,
And stifle all their earnest doubt,
Were but the parody of faith:
They dare not cheat their common sense

With that evasive reverence
Which still denies below its breath.
They shudder at the rash belief
That sides with the majority,
And hires with a retaining fee
Glib advocates who hold a brief,
Perhaps believing in their cause,
But pledged beforehand, confident,
And less truth-seekers than intent
On winning orthodox applause.

So, in the too fastidious vein
Engender'd by a life recluse
In which misgiving grows with use,
I hear a pensive voice complain :—

" So often it has come to pass !
" Each age the futile hope renews :
" In vain humanity pursues
" Some will-o'-wisp across the grass,
" To go more hopelessly astray.
" The legends of the dreaming past

" Were beautiful, but faded fast.

" As in the growing heat of day,

" The floating mists upon the plain

" Dissolve to airy nothingness,

" So all the vague unreal bliss

" Had gleamed upon the world in vain.

" The Heaven that had stooped to earth

" Was as a thing that once had been :

" For ever gone the radiant scene,

" The stately music and the mirth,

" The choral dance and festival,

" The long processions of the priests :

" They could not banish from their feasts

" The hand that wrote upon the wall

" To tell them they had had their day.

" The mystic influence that played

" So great a part, the law obeyed

" That dooms the brightest to decay.

" The faith that had so long prevailed

" Was like a tree whose sap runs out :

" Swept by the icy blast of doubt,

" Its leaf and tender fruitage failed.

"The seers looked, but could not see;

"Attendant nymphs of stream or grove

"Forsook their haunts, and ceased to rove;

"The world was tired of fantasy.

"The Oracles some dumbness sealed:

"Their wisdom was discredited;

"Their double-dealing words, 'twas said,

"Had hidden rather than revealed.

"The Bacchic frenzy and the song

"That thinly veiled the naked lust

"Subsided; prostrate in the dust

"The superstition potent long.

"The flamens and the vestals all

"Have left but ashes in their urns,

"As dust to merely dust returns

"In sad and hopeless burial.

"No worshippers libations pour,

"For all the mighty gods are dead.

"The visionary scene has fled;

"Their places know them now no more.

"Yet, since the hunger of the heart

"Was strong, and cried to be appeased

" The vanished forms the Sculptor seized,

" And still immortalised in Art.

" His plastic hand incarnated,

" Though in a kind of mimicry,

" The gods that mortals fain would see ;

" But the inspiring faith was dead.

" The artist could not animate

" The glorious forms his hand could mould,

" The marble was so deadly cold,

" But glorified their lost estate.

" What then was left for man whereto

" His soul might turn itself for food ?

" The fleeting forms of earthly good

" Might satisfy the swinish crew

" Who seek no paradise but earth ;

" But, with a nobler ardour fired,

" The purer spirits still aspired

" To claim the honours of their birth.

" Some read the stars, and thought they saw

" In movements of the complex choir

" How things in heaven and earth conspire,

" And all our life is veiled in awe.

" But Who, or where, or what is He

" Whose will the wheeling choirs obey,

" No wisest of the seers could say ;

" Their unknown God was Destiny.

" The heart was empty, and a chill

" Reaction after baffled zeal,

" Where death had almost set its seal,

" Had fallen on the hopeless will.

" Philosophy then filled the void ;

" Through Plato and his glorious school

" The worship of the beautiful,

" Which doubt had daunted, not destroyed,

" Arose again—its best result

" A more ideal turn of thought.

" The archetype the thinker sought

" Was found, and in the Christian cult

" Philosophy joined hand in hand

" With faith, to give the world a creed.

" The gulf of being seemed indeed

" If this were true, completely spanned.

" If I could think it wholly true

" That One has come by moving sign

" To prove the roots of life divine,

" And lead us by a certain clue,

" All life were happier ; but I see

" How Hope creates a Paradise,

" And how the airy visions rise

" Of God and immortality.

" To take our place among the gods

" Immortal in beatitude—

" To see in Him, the Perfect Good,

" The mighty Jove who never nods,

" And to discover after all

" That we have only claspt a cloud !

" The lower for our dreamings proud

" The idol we had raised would fall.

" Far better, surely, to await

" The great event that none foresee :

" Perhaps a God of love may be,

" And not a mere relentless Fate :

" I know not, and I deem it best

" To trace again the characters

" Which Moses reads amiss or blurs,

" On Nature's wondrous palimpsest.

"The elements have made their mark,
" And Science with a certain rule
" Can measure all : in that great school
" To honest learners nought is dark.
" I work by methods well defined,
" But all that lies beyond their range
" Is doubtful: men's opinions change ;
" No age is of a constant mind.
" Yet, though illusions fade and flee,
" There stands one sure and stedfast rock
" Immovable amid the shock
" Of waves upon a restless sea.
" All nature owns the reign of law :
" There they who look may clearly see:
" All else is merely drapery
" To clothe the human hope and awe.
" The wish was father to the thought :
" The gods of old came down to men :
" A human god might come again :
" What wonder if to minds untaught
" Some grand heroic Man might show
" Such wisdom, mastery, and force,

" And eloquence of pure discourse,

" That, as they watch its golden flow,

" They own Him noble and divine ?

" A hero, demigod, or more,

" He comes the Order to restore

" Long passed away ; and with the wine

" Of new belief they fain would fill

" The bottles that had waxen old,

" Unfit the larger truth to hold,

" Till by an effort of their will

' Their hope has grown into a creed.

" On that unreal basis stands

" The ' house of God not made with hands.'

" The Christian witnesses agreed,

" But who can trust their ears and eyes ?

" Through men so simple and devout

" Who know not what it is to doubt,

The worst delusions may arise."

This attitude might answer well

If we could stand outside ourselves,

And thoughts were merely tricksome elves

Like those that haunt some fairy dell,
And so dismiss as poetry—
A toiling life's Midsummer dream—
The more ethereal lights that gleam
Across the earthly scenery.
If men could live within the seen
And find their nature satisfied,
With patience we might then abide
Till death shall come to shift the scene.
But when, within us, deep to deep
In storms of Passion loudly calls,
When conscience speaks, and sin appals,
And fears we cannot lay to sleep
Make us demand the reason why
Of this unrest ; and though the dust
Casts blindness on us, and though lust
Debases, yet within us cry
Pure voices coming from afar,
And, as a harp by sweet airs swept,
We hear the harmonies that are
Within us, and around, to bear
Their witness of our heritage,

We burst the bars of this poor cage,
And soar into our proper air.

And even Science must believe,
And almost blindly, some few things:
The warp and woof of proof are strings
That only Faith can strongly weave.
All reasonings of men must start
From something that commands assent:
The cogency of argument
Is more than dialetic art.
The instruments by which we think
We must believe in, and the whole
Complex machine we call the soul
Is like a chain whose every link
The thinker cannot choose but trust,
And, though his sight is often dim,
The reason that is given him
He uses freely, lest it rust.
Presentiments that come unsought
Press onwards through some open gate:
Though ambushed Error lie in wait,

The birthright of a man is Thought.

'Twas Malebranche, the sage, who said—

" *Attention is a prayer for light ;*"

The thinker, when he thinks aright,

Is heard and answered in his need.

No traveller has found the source

Where springs the Life that in its course

The earthly tributaries feed,

But all the lands through which it flows

Are gladdened by the gracious stream.

As mountain-tops that cloud-capt seem

Pour down their wealth of melting snows,

So, from a thousand rivers fed,

The stream of knowledge gathers force,

And bears its freight of high discourse,

To souls of men like living bread.

To us the world is full of light,

Since all created things are signs

Whose inner meaning man divines:

We walk by faith and not by sight.

The mystic origin of man

Grows clearer as our mother Earth

Shows tokens to us of our birth,
Not here amid the dust of Time,
But in the dim Eternity.
To heights where life is large and free
These feet of ours shall one day climb;
For from the Infinite there come
Such wafts of love, such passionate
Prognostic of our true estate,
Such listenings of faith, and dumb
Out-reachings of the soul to God,
That we are here as men that dream,
And in transfigured moments seem
To tread where angels may have trod.

We slept in feeble infancy,
But who shall tell what visions came,
Not shadowed yet by thoughts of shame?
One Face the children always see.
Sometimes our life seems all a dream:
The eyes that opened on the earth
Were wistful, for the hour of birth
Is like the springing of a stream

That hastens to a distant Sea
Which man sees dimly from afar
And, like the Magi, seeks a star
To guide him till the shadows flee.
From one belief his course must start,
That truth is at the root of things ;
His thoughts are the awakenings
Of spirit-being, each a part
Of one great whole ; and being so,
From truth to truth he finds his way,
And hails the tokens of the day,
As certainties take form and grow.
The ground is firm beneath his feet
Because his human faculties
He trusts.   Existence, wanting this,
Were only one prolonged deceit.
But fear dilates his startled eyes
To see unveiled the Master's hand ;
As one who cannot understand
Is speechless in his great surprise,
He fears the play of some false light
From dreamland, and would shut it out.

So ignorance engenders doubt,

But Faith can read the sign aright.

How can the scornful doubter know

That miracle is breach of law ?

The men who tell us what they saw

By no means write their record so.

The forms appearing on the scene

Our infant sciences transcend,*

Yet may they show that pathways tend

Where only feet divine have been.

The broken Order that we see

Is not the highest, after all ;

A Mind all-seeing could forestall

The gropings of futurity.

Our human methods are so slow ;

But what if all the secret things

We track through painful reasonings

He doth not need to seek, but know ?

His eye a wider field may scan,

And, touching springs of life more deep,

---

*Appendix A.

C

Within a law of nature keep
Still hidden from the ken of man.
If Science could do half as much
In ages, as in those three years
He did, Whose word unstopp'd deaf ears
And healed the palsied with a touch,
It might with more of fair pretence
Adopt that proud omniscient tone
Which in this century has grown
To almost haughty insolence.

We own the range of Nature's laws,
And yet we know the will behind
The published edict shows a Mind
Whose being speaks in every clause.
The mystic power can none escape
That thrills creation with its awe :
The great World-Artist works by law
To mould the matter into shape.
And in His workshop you shall see
The product of His plastic skill
In living forms ; on plain and hill

There is a breath of mystery,
As if there stood behind the veil
A Presence greater far than all
The mountain heights whose shadows fall
At eventide, adown the dale.
Dim-eyed, we are not wholly blind;
There passes over Nature's face
A fugitive celestial grace
Some inward instinct has divined.
So sensitive in soul we are!
This quicken'd kindredness between
Our nature and the outer scene,
Is like a message sent from far.
At best our Science knows in part,
And, searching though its eager gaze,
Its certainty is but a phrase—
The clouds of truth so slowly part!
For how the grass upon the lawns
First came, the wisest doth not know,
Or how the thoughts within us grow,
Or how the childish reason dawns.
Much lieth hidden from our quest:

We cannot sound the mystic deep,

Or span the Heavens, in the sweep

Of seeing at its very best.

Man measures, weighs, and deeply thinks,

Asks certainty, but asks in vain ;

He cannot tell who forged the chain

Of which he sees the latest links.

He cannot tell, for, out of sight,

And long anterior to life,

Arose the elemental strife

With Chaos and the realm of Night.

If, in the trackless ages past,

Creation's path in shadow lies,

And Science vainly strains her eyes

To pierce the gloom ; if questions asked

Get nothing but a half-reply

That pregnant question of the soul—

The moral meaning of the whole—

For which the constant ages cry,

When sages falter in their speech,

God stoops in mercy to reveal.

As men in blindness grope, to feel

If through the darkness they can reach
Some sure support on which to rest,
So we, whose hungry wand'ring glance
Is checked by walls of ignorance,
Would deem our life indeed unblest
If never, from the great unknown
From which we come, to which we go,
Could silence break to make us know
We are not straws by wild winds strown
On streams that lose themselves in sand—
To make articulate the sighs
Of strong desire, the spirit-cries
That rise, and pass from land to land—
To tell us what there is of true
In dim suggestions that arise,
And lead us on from vague surmise
Till certainty is full in view.
If God is God, and men are men,
The shadow of the Infinite
Will fall, and lead us on from IT
To HIM who in the deep Amen
Of human life is satisfied—

Who gave us for our life His breath,
And leads us through the gate of death
To see the things the shadows hide.

This discontent, these passionate
Attempts of ours to seize and hold
The truths the forms of language mould,—
This thirst that nothing seems to sate
To know the very truth of things,
Might serve to show us that the soul
Was meant at last to know the whole
Of which it has foreshadowings.
The range of human thought is more
Than all our symbols can express;
The wisest of our race confess
That they are standing on the shore,
Mere wistful gazers on a sea
Which stretches far beyond their reach,
And struggle in imperfect speech
To set their pent emotion free.
Although their nobler works may live,
The perfect form of art was miss'd,

And what they did they hardly wist.
So, in the poet's sensitive
And tender touch of feeling's chords,
A vision of some greater thing
Than all his best imagining
Eludes the baffled grasp of words.
And this ideal which transcends
All art, all mortal eloquence,
Belongs not to the world of sense.
Eternal Wisdom condescends
To train us in an earthly school,
Sustains our ardour of desire,
Through these rude forms would lead us higher,
To know the Good, the Beautiful.

Say that our life is incomplete :
If truth be at the root of all,
Though one by one the thinkers fall,
This lifelong passionate heart-beat
Is one of nature's prophecies
Of what our life is meant to be.
The artist fairer forms shall see

When truth immortal clears his eyes.
No side-glance at the Perfect Truth,
But comes from Him, the Source of good,
By whom our thoughts are understood ;
And through the dreamings of.our youth,
In hope, desire, presentiment,
He communes with us, to forecast
The truth that shall be known at last,
As something yet more excellent.

But this, some say, is dreaming too:
They fain would touch and handle all
The feelings as they rise and fall,
The lights and shadows on the view
Thought tries to seize, but soon lets slip.
This Nature has so many things,
Mere "fallings from us, vanishings,"
Which all the cunning of the lip
Can ill interpret to our thought.
But there were surely tokens there
Of something so divinely fair,
Suggested, hinted, hardly caught,

That life grows tame and commonplace
From which the hope it kindled fades,
And all the beauty of the glades
Has lost its spiritual grace.

But, though the poet-nature feels
Within his soul, and everywhere,
A Spirit moving in the air,
Which sense half hides, and half reveals,
And walks as if on holy ground,
The duller men of coarser grain
Deride such fancies, and complain
That this is merely empty sound.
Too practical to dream or muse,
They treat it as a grave offence
Disparaging to common sense,
To let imagination loose.
Well, let us take our common stand
On lower levels.   We are awed
By tokens, as we look abroad,
Of more than sense can understand.

If they must judge by rule of touch,
And ask the questions "Where?" and "When?"—
The force that swayed the wills of men
And left on History so much
Of substance—let them ponder it.
The passion that could fire the cold,
And make the timorous high-souled,
As men whose aims were infinite—
Had this its root in fantasy?
How could they make their goings sure?
How could the works they did endure?
What bond of real unity,
What hope for right against the wrong,
To make the way of progress clear,
But faith in God, who giveth ear
To them who cry—"*How long? how long?*"
Were there no central ground for men,
No bond to bind us into one,
No Ruler seated on His throne,
Why should not anarchy again
Sweep like a tidal wave o'er all
That out of chaos men have won?

Historic unity undone,
The future with the past would fall.
Beneath the internecine strife,
The forward movement, and the chill
That often fell upon the will,
The prophets saw a cosmic life,
And sometimes, in exulting strains,
Appealed to all who would be free,
And led them on to victory,
Until they rose and broke their chains.

Yet, since there mingle Nature's cry
And earth-born thought with things divine,
And we can hardly mark the line
Where hopes and fears of men that die
Break in, and mar the prophet's strain—
Since our interpretations fail,
And men would see without its veil
The truth of God, to read it plain—
There grew a hope so strong and clear
That nations dwelling far apart

Who press'd it to their beating heart,

Thrilled strangely as the hour drew near.

It grew into a raging thirst

That nothing seemed to satisfy,

For all the reservoirs were dry

That seemed so promising at first—

Would God Himself but speak to man !

At last the standard was unfurled

That stirred the heart of all the world,

And through the lands the tidings ran—

" Lo, He hath come, the world's desire

" To smite the battlements of wrong !"

Hearts beat again, and hands grow strong ;

Despairing wills once more aspire

To scale the heights of saintliness,

And making light of suffering,

And counting life a little thing,

By deathless deeds to glory press.

The world leapt up with life renewed,

And all the future glowed with light,

When, longing faith replaced by sight,

He came to lead the hosts of good.

The men that, wandering forlorn,
Had been as children fatherless,
Knelt down, since He had come to bless,
And all the unbelieving scorn
Of mocking spirits only drew
The children closer to the side
Of Him whose breath had purified
The hope that now sprang up anew.

Then some who scoffed began to pray,
They found that now, baptised with fire,
The resurrection of desire
Was sweeter for the long delay.
The wilderness and desert smiled,
New flowers of grace began to grow,
And busy husbandmen to sow
The seed that would reclaim the wild.

Coherent grew the life of man;
The many strong conflicting wills
Together flowed, like mountain rills
That into one great channel ran.
The sense of brotherhood was dim
Till He who showed by word and sign

How human life becomes divine
United all through love of Him.
And this great thought is living still ;
The doubters who, whate'er their plea,
In every man a brother see,
Must follow Christ against their will.
And some who yield to that constraint,
Not knowing wherefore they obey,
By many speaking signs bewray
The secret temper of the saint.*
They enter not the Temple gate,
But from the Holy City strains
Have strayed, that, floating o'er the plains,
Have reached them in their sad estate.
There is a blessing on the meek
Who, though they doubt, nor strive nor cry,
And still for clearer vision sigh.
Their love is strong if faith is weak,
And they who love are more akin
To Him who sums Himself in this,

---

* Appendix B.

Than dreamers on a selfish bliss,
Who only care that they may win.
The puzzles of the intellect
Are known to Him who knoweth man,
And, in the working of His plan,
Perhaps among His own elect
Some sad misgiving souls may be,
Who, walking with uncertain tread,
Have through the darkness still been led;
For all the pure in heart shall see!

The Nightfall.*

THE Sun, slow vanishing, hath set,
   But darkness deepeneth not yet.
These trembling movements of the light
Forewarn us now that stealthy Night
Is near, and all things feel her breath :
A form like that of hooded Death
Is putting forth a dusky hand
To dim the beauty of the land.
These faint vibrations in the air
Are like a sympathetic scare,
As if a soul beneath the sense
Discerned a hostile influence.

Like Autumn, lovely in decay,
So fades the glory of the day.

* Appendix C.

Long streams of crimson from the west
Show glorious on the mountain's crest;
But in an instant passes too
The spendour of that roseate hue.
Then, shooting through the afterglow,
Some magic hath the skill to throw
Long darts of light, that change to gold
Each edge of cloud; and o'er the wold
The floating mist is all aflame.
As when some grave and stately dame
Lights up the pallour of her hue
With rosebuds, sprinkled as with dew,
So Nature o'er the azure throws
A vesture rich with evening glows,
And wears, in southern splendour drest,
One cross of brilliants on her breast.

But Twilight now uplifts her hand,
And as she waves her fairy wand,
All forms are melted and transfused;
The gazer, hardly disabused
Of all that lately dazzled him,

D

Yet sees the glory waxen dim.

Night darkens swiftly on the sky,

And all things seem to heave a sigh

Of grief, to think the day is dead.

And, as men walk with soften'd tread

In presence of that great repose

When, sad at heart, some watcher throws

In tenderness the decent veil

To hide the face, so marble pale,

So now upon the rev'rent breast

There falls a solemn sense of rest.

When all the west has lost its glow,

With steps grown pensive now, and slow,

The wanderer, absorbed in thought,

Amid the gloom has faintly caught

Some vague suggestion in the hour

Of converse with a holy Power.

The darkling glade is filled with peace:

As one who welcomes the release

From garish day, and gauds of sense,

He bendeth low in reverence.

Ephphàtha.

TONGUE-TIED and deaf, his speech was pent,
    And yet his eyes were eloquent
With plaintive thought:—
        " The people seem
" Fantastic figures in a dream :
" I see them, but I cannot hear
" The voice that speaks to me good cheer.
" As soon as born, each accent dies :
" I lose myself in vain surmise
" To see one glad expression chase
" Another o'er the speaking face,
" Now bright, and now so tender grown—
" Among them all I dwell alone.

" I watch the rain-drops from the eaves,
" I see the trembling of the leaves,
" The rushing of the waterfall.

" The air, they say, is musical,

" But, though its motion I can see,

" What is there musical to me ?

" The Ocean, eloquent in speech,

" May pour upon the shingly beach

" Its wondrous, ever-varying tale :

" I neither hear the shrieking gale,

" The sudden crash, the hollow boom,

" Nor thunder like the crack of doom.

" I see, but cannot understand

" The life and movement on the strand.

" A lonely man amid the crowd

" I wander ever, moody-browed,

" Shut up from men within the cell

" Of solitary thought.　The spell

" Upon my sense I cannot break :

" I seem like one but half awake.

" Whilst other senses thrill to hear

" The voices that are silver clear,

" And tones of love that touch the heart,

" From this I stand a man apart.

" All life is like a barren plain :

' My soul is dry : shall no soft rain

" To make the flowers of feeling grow

" Till blessèd tears of gladness flow,

" Fall from the breaking clouds of speech ?

" Far as the weary eye can reach

" One arid waste of life is seen

" On which can flourish nothing green.

" No dew of tender feeling falls,

" No voice of fond affection calls,

" No interchange of thought can bless

" The deaf man in his loneliness.

" And nowhere am I lonelier

" Than when, amid the city's stir,

" I wander on through silent streets.

" No voice the hapless pilgrim greets :

" Not men but spectres pass me by.

" Ah, no ! the deaf see all awry :

" The men are living, but to me

" Their life is utter mystery,

" And mine to them.   The plaintive look

" They cast on me, as on a book

" In cypher, that they cannot read,

" Betrays to each a common need,

" As if their love, like mine, were bound.

" So, on some broken bridge of sound

" Two brothers stretch across the void,

" The pathway of their thought destroyed :

" Their parted lives can never meet,

" Though heart to heart may truly beat.

" To them the living world is dumb :

" Between them gestures go and come

" That do but tantalise the sight

" With visions of a lost delight."

So in the moving crowd he stood,

His life a mournful solitude.

But Jesus, as He passed him by,

Interpreted the sad soul cry,

And in an instant all was changed.

So long from human kind estranged,

He took again his proper place,

On equal terms with all his race.

The world, so inarticulate,

Now spake to him.   The closèd gate
On which sweet sounds had fallen dead
The Lord unbarr'd.   One word He said,
And that one word had made him free
Of all the wealth of land and sea;
In Nature's songs, so many-voiced,
As one newborn the man rejoiced.

Not he alone whose open brow
The day salutes, is vocal now.
It seems as if the tongue-tied earth
Had broken into sudden mirth,
Yet with a touch of pathos too,
Like flowers whose eyes are wet with dew.
The tinkling bells across the lea,
The voices coming from the sea,
The winds that seem to sigh and wail
Among the hills, or in the vale,
The sound of softly falling rain,
The lowing cattle on the plain,
Or yonder, by the river's edge,
The water lapping in the sedge,

Or, in the woods. the melody
The growing light of day sets free,
The evening sounds that lull to sleep,
Or those when Nature seems to weep
When darkness falleth upon all
Alike to him are musical.
He hardly understands his bliss,
Surrounded by such mysteries.
So much his eye had failed to see!
He listens to the lullaby
With which the Ocean rocks to rest
The white-winged creatures on her breast;
The distant forest muttering
To him seems like a living thing
That, rooted to the ground, must still
The air with its remonstrance fill.
The breeze that waves the rustling corn,
The echoes of the hunter's horn,
The hum of honey-laden bees,
The secrets whispered by the trees,
The solemn cawing of the rooks,
And, nestling in leafy nooks,

The love-bird calling to her mate—
He hears them all; they satiate
His baulk'd desire to hear the song
Of Nature that was dumb so long.

Then human life, grown vocal, came
About his heart; he was the same
And yet so changed! For now he heard
Voices with deep emotion stirr'd,
And, in their cadences of tone,
He who had dwelt so long alone
Could enter into fellowship
With thoughts that pass from lip to lip.
Upon the laughter and the glee
He looked not now so wistfully.
He heard the murmur of the throng,
And when there came a burst of song
From singing women, and the strain
Of minstrelsy, 'twas almost pain
From its exceeding ecstasy,
To feel his spirit ranging free
On heights where only prophets tread,

Through all the maze of music led.
And pathos, too, appealed to him
Whose eyes had once, confused and dim,
Observed and watched, as one amazed
To see the features fall, and gazed
Perplexed at grief that seemed so deep.
He now could weep with them that weep,
And learnt how men are comforted
When bending even o'er their dead.

If by and by to him shall come
A change to make him once more dumb,
And there shall fall unbroken sleep
As when the heavy opiates steep
The clouded over-burdened sense,
Yet none need tremble in suspense.
The darkness gone, again will live
The soul, made quick and sensitive;
Embodied with a rarer skill
Will thought through nobler organs thrill.
No halting tongue and no deaf ears
To risen men through all the years!

The Christian Passover.

NOT with bitter herbs of rue
   Keep we now the Paschal Feast;
There has risen into view,
   In the Christian Eucharist,
Much that in the old time past
   Lay in shadow; and to faith
Life is evident at last
   Deeper and more strong than death.
Though there mingle even here,
   In our sad mortality,
Thoughts that wear a robe of fear,
   They will pass, and leave us free.
Waiting here, with staff in hand,
   Girded, feasting as in haste,
When our Leader shall command
   We will pass across the waste.

None shall stumble there, or faint ;
　Through the night our journey lies,
On the starlit firmament
　Gazing with our solemn eyes.
But the pilgrim songs are sweet
　That beguile us as we go :
Well the path that holy feet
　Trod in ages past, we know.
In the dim uncertain light
　We can see the marks they set :
Through the watches of the night,
　Though the dawning tarries yet,
Thronging round us as we pass,
　Spirits guard us that can see
What is dim to us—alas !—
　Earth's and Heaven's unity.
Mystic voices in the air
　Thrill us with their tenderness,
And a look of light they wear
　As they bid us onward press.
Comfortable words are said,
　And the feeble heart grows bold—

Jesus liveth who was dead !
  Never can His love grow cold.
With the food that is divine
  Of the holy wayside Feast,
And the water and the wine,
  He doth feed us, King and Priest.
In the true immortal life
  Better food He gives than this :
Here, the terror and the strife,
  There, the settled calm of bliss.
By this way of pilgrimage
  All who long for Him must go—
Saint and Sinner, Seer and Sage.
  There are prayers soft and low
Helping us upon our way :
  There are hero-voices too.
Noble words and strong they say :—
  " Thou art faithful, Thou art true :
" Thou hast borne for us Thy Cross ;
  " Whom Thou lovest—they are blest.
" What is earthly gain or loss
  " If in Thee we find our rest ?

" Saviour, may we learn of Thee

   "Till Thy yoke grows light indeed,

" Though we share Thine Agony,

   " And the wounded heart may bleed."

The Widow's Son of Nain.

" He saith to her : Weep not."

HOW could she choose but weep
　　When he who was her only son
Lay there in his last sleep—
Of all her loved ones left not one?
How could she but recall
Her early days of widowhood,
When winter fell on all,
And woman's young beatitude
Had passed like any dream?
One thing alone her life sustained—
In gloom one bright sun-gleam—
Her son, her comforter, remained.

And now that son is dead!
The lifeless form upon the bier

They bear to its last bed.
If ever one might shed a tear
That one was surely she.
The heart's complaint we almost hear—
" *O son, not weep for thee,*
" *Who wert, and art, so dear, so dear !* "

Who would not feel for her ?
The Stranger bids the bearers stay,
And they, without demur,
In great astonishment obey.
They see upon His face
A look of strange unearthly power,
And yet a human grace.
So tender of her wither'd flower,
He understands her woe,
And speaks His gracious words of cheer
In accents soft and low
That fall like music on the ear.
What depth of holy light
Is looking from those wondrous eyes,
So soft and yet so bright !

Then, when He bids the youth arise
The dead comes back again,
Like to a sleeper who awakes,
Roused by the hum of men.
A holy voice the silence breaks
With words of happy sound.
" *Why should you weep ? He is not dead !*
" *He lives ! the lost is found.*"
Not now with mournful muffled tread
The slow procession goes.
The blood is mounting to his cheek,
The heavy eyes unclose ;
The lately dead begins to speak,
The fetter'd mind is free.
The strains of plaintive music cease,
The minstrel melody
That bids the soul depart in peace.
The beckon'd soul returns ;
The vital spark that had decayed
Is lit again, and burns ;
And now they burst in praise who prayed.

E

He had not wandered far
But on the verge of Paradise
Where happy spirits are,
Had lingered, in his great surprise
To see the form they wear,
And hardly for a little hour
Could breathe that finer air,
But, like a man bereft of power,
Saw all as one that dreamed—
So strangely through the slumb'rous sense
The mystic glory gleamed.

And yet that breath of innocence
Would sweeten now to him
The life of earth he had to live.
One moment on the brim
Of life more deep, more sensitive
To every touch of good,
The man who almost with the blest
A little while had stood,
And seen their perfectness of rest,
Would bear with him through all
Some sign upon his very face

Of what that interval
Had wrought for him of growth in grace.

Mysterious wave of life
That breaks upon these earthly shores
With foam of grief and strife !
Its goings vainly love explores.
As moonlight grows and wanes
We see the strong tides ebb and flow ;
We hear the mingling strains
Of gladness fading into woe.
Across the waves of sound
Pass cries for help or sad farewell,
And each sepulchral mound
Some tragic history might tell.
The cry was answered then ;
The springs of life were out of sight,
But now there flowed again
A fuller stream of pure delight.

Ah, what is He who stands,
Ideal greatness in His face,
And with uplifted hands,

E 2

Like one of a superior race ?
They know not whence He came,
Or where He gat His royalty,
But on the roll of fame
Is none inscribed so great as He.
For He hath made it plain
That Life is lordliest of all,
And despot Death in vain
To his destroying hosts shall call
To raise his fallen crown.
The souls of men of right belong
To Him who once laid down
The life that was so great and strong.

Men live, they fade, they die,
They gather weeping round the grave,
But not in vain they cry—
He will restore the life He gave.
All lips once cold in death
His kiss of love will touch, and then
His vivifying breath
Will change the dead to living men.

The Star in the East.

1.

UNCERTAIN of all things, and still in its youth,
 The world had its teachers, who saw in the sky
The portents and signs of a kingdom of Truth,
 And a hope for mankind that never can die.

2.

Those tremblings of light, in the darkest of ages,
 Seen dimly, as seen when men look from afar,
In the mystical east, by scholars and sages,
 Were heralds to tell of the King and His Star.

3.

Not one but repeated epiphanies come
 In answer to thoughts that unbidden arise
From depths of reflection, and lips that were dumb
 Are touched as by fire at the words of the wise.

4.

Though languages vary, the nature is one;
　In the glass of its thought is mirror'd the Face
The world had so longed for; each epoch begun
　Enlarges to faith the horizon of grace.

5.

And often, when men have been dreaming their
　　dreams,
　Unconscious that near is the breaking of day,
And hardly discerning what *is* from what seems,
　The shadow was falling of One on His way.

6.

Each leader of men to the Truth is a Seer
　To whom have been opened some vistas of light:
If ever their visions seem growing more clesr,
　The Christ that is coming but looms through
　　the night.

7.

Himself He eternally utters in speech:
　The voices inspired that the ages have heard
Are echoes of something yet greater, since each
　Has felt in his soul a Revealer, The Word.

8.

Still strengthens and grows the immortal desire:
　Though clouded by passion, and daunted by fear,
Yet kindled again, it burns on with a higher
　And purer emotion, and Heaven draws near.

9.

The hopes that were dying have risen again
　First mutter'd in legend and saga and song,
Then spoken in promise, until among men
　He cometh, the King who has tarried so long.

Judas Iscariot.

ENEATH the story of his flight
    There sounds a solemn undertone
Of deeper meaning. *It was night !* *
Disciple into traitor grown,
The pulses of his life beat low.
Like one upon a precipice
O'erhanging an abyss of woe,
Who trembles lest he tread amiss,
A thought of fear has chilled his blood.
The dread he dared not speak aloud
Is with him in his solitude :
There darkness wraps him like a shroud.

The Feast had lingered, and the tone
Of sorrow in the Master's speech

---

* St. John xiii., 30.

Had sounded almost like a moan,
As, looking solemnly at each,
He seemed to search the inmost heart
Of every guest, that paschal night.
We see the horror and the start
Of sudden wondering affright.
The crisis of His cause drew nigh,
And now upon their fervent zeal
Had come this solemn prophecy,
Love's last, pathetic, pure appeal.
What wonder if a shadow fell?
Who was the traitor at his post?
Some man who stood as sentinel,
Perhaps the servant trusted most.
Half doubtful of their innocence
We hear them murmur their dismay
With feeling that has grown intense.
And Judas—why does he delay?
A guilty man, the time has come
To penetrate his thin disguise,
And treachery is stricken dumb
Before those sad, reproachful eyes.

They know him now : the choice is made,
And, as he goeth to betray,
Too late to warn him, or upbraid.
His footfall, as it dies away,
Has lost its tread of manly faith :
Out in the night they seem to see
The panic in the panting breath
Of him who gropes so guiltily,
While through the leaves the night-wind sighs.
He knows not what the fear, or where,
But every step forebodes surprise
From terrors moving in the air.

The clouds have gathered, and the sky
The peaceful paschal moon had lit
Is mantled now in mystery.
No moonlight gleams ; no shadows flit.
The night has grown so deadly still
Through which the lonely spirit strays !
On him the dews no balm distil,
But thoughts of merely wild amaze
Have risen, like a silent host,

And conscience cowers, sore afraid.
So, on the lonely moor, one lost
With sinking heart despairs of aid,
And hour by hour more surely knows
The worst he feared has come to pass.
No sign can tell him, as he goes,
How near may be the deep morass.
Why did he cast the lamp away
To wander on, without a guide,
On this wild moor, where marshlights play,
Or in the darkness pitfalls hide?

This sudden strange obscurity
Is surely more than Nature's gloom.
This silence, too! So silently
Steal on the messengers of doom.
Can life itself be closing in?
With feet of wool pursueth Fate:
Right in the track of mortal sin
Do stern avengers always wait?
What fleeting tender memories
May then have come to plead with him,

Of happy days when on his bliss
No breath had come to make it dim !
All that is over now and gone :
With lying promises of power
The mocking spirits lure him on—
He is the man, and this the hour !

So false of heart, he once was true,
But, fretting sorely at delay,
His fretfulness to treason grew.
He never could forget the day
When he, a man of Kerioth,
Had followed Christ with ardent faith,
And pledged to Him this broken troth.
He heard, as one who held his breath,
The words that soared beyond his reach,
Yet won his fealty.   Inspired
By that strange music of His speech
Of which who heard Him never tired
He saw the light and owned it sweet,
And, shielded by His glorious power,
Adventured on with fearless feet

To wait with Him His coming hour.

But there had grown a harder mood

When nothing came of all this talk.

He saw the Lord in silence brood,

He saw Him still in Jewry walk,

And nothing yet at all fulfilled

The hope that drew him to His side,

No deed on which a man could build.

And, whether 'twas with wounded pride,

Or low ambition baulk'd and foiled,

Or some indulged and secret sin,

He plotted as a man despoiled

Of something he had hoped to win.

Then love in that disciple died :

Then woke to life the meaner soul ;

The lust that would not be denied

Had trampled down his weak control,

And when he made his final choice,

The Tempter claimed him for his own.

Then ceased the warnings of the voice

Which none had heard save he alone,

And purer eyes than men's might see

There, at his side, a vacant place,
Where once his angel tenderly
Had plied his ministry of grace.

From him whose aims so high had soared
The guardian of his soul had fled.
To see the precious ointment poured
So freely, on that Sacred Head,
By one whose love, forgetting self, *
Gave all, and with an instinct fine,
To gold transmuted worldly pelf
Inflamed to wrath his thought malign.
"*Such criminal and senseless waste*
"*Would ruin any enterprise!*"
As one who rashly had embraced
A cause, and now with clearer eyes
Sees all is lost, and in despair
Deplores his rash resolve too late,
He leaves them, if they will, to share
Their fond delusion, and their fate.
He goes, and will return no more:

* St. John xii., 3-5.

The traitor is unmasked at last—
Can they forget the look he wore
When forth into the night he passed ?
What was it ? Grief, or lurking hate ?
Or merely passionate farewell ?
One passing gleam with hope elate,
And then the gloomy features fell.

Is all as patent as it seems
In this old Galilæan tale ?
It furnishes so many themes
For declamation, but they fail
Through looking only on the shell
And husk of things : the traitor's mind
Had shiftings more than those they tell—
The tangled skein the few unwind.
Disciple and evangelist
Record the tale of his offence,
And yet perhaps they hardly wist
The whole, or else some reticence
Of tenderness their hand restrained ;
From graver faults they turn aside

To dwell upon the pity feigned.

But there had been a rising tide

Of worldly feeling in them all

That drifted them upon its breast :

If his was a profounder fall,

His danger had beset the rest.

The most devoted of the band*

Had been as one who wrought for hire,

Though no dishonour stained his hand.

How self may mingle with desire

The most heroic in its aim,

And tend to make the life untrue,

And all the growth of goodness maim,

The holiest amongst them knew.

That death of self is gain of life

It took them weary years to know :

They saw not that their sorest strife

Would be with an unearthly foe.

In time they started in affright,

As men upon a mountain ledge

---

* St. Matthew, xix., 27.

Who walk in some deceiving light
Recoil when near the giddy edge :
One farther step were certain death.
But he had tottered to his fall
Before one voice, with trembling breath,
Could sound the terrified recall.
The solemn ages, as they pass,
See shuddering a human form
With face upturned upon the grass,
Like one who perished in the storm
That gathered round him in the wild—
No eye to pity, none to save,
No love that on his childhood smiled
To lay him gently in the grave.
What lieth there is senseless clay :
The schemes, the dreams of life are done :
O shut thine eyes, pure light of day !
And draw thy veil, thou setting Sun !

Some kind of faith he may have had,
No trustful, self-subjecting will,
Ennobled when the heart is sad,

Inspired and strengthened by the thrill
That animates for sacrifice,
But some remains of dull belief
That may presume, when ardour dies,
To basely serve the chosen Chief,
And, hoping always against hope,
Would urge him on by deeds to show
His purpose of a larger scope
Long treasured, and to strike the blow.
As one who thought with sleight of hand
To fool the Sanhedrim at last,
With evil craft but aspect bland
His loaded dice the traitor cast.
The man must dare whose feet would climb:
The Christ might triumph, though betrayed,
And triumph would condone his crime.
The promised Kingdom, long delayed,
Would surely come ; His foes would see
That all their boasted power and pride
Had shrivelled into vanity,
Their vengeance foiled, their hopes belied.
And he who hastened on the deed,

No longer hated and reviled,

Would take his place of power, and plead

As one on whom a King hath smiled.

In dark recesses of his soul

Some remnant of ignoble faith

Might harbour, and the distant goal

Show dimly through the mists of death.

The paltry pieces they had flung

Like offal to a prowling dog—

Were *they* the prize?   He saw a Throne

And Kingdom looming through the fog.

For ever, through that weary time,

There sounded a triumphal note;

He daily conn'd the words sublime,

Like some hard lesson learnt by rote.

To see HIM, with His royal glance,

Dispense His offices of State,

Yet give no order to advance,

Stirr'd passions that were almost hate.

" *Twelve Thrones* "—Twelve princes would **arise***

---

* St. Matthew, xix., 28.

To rule and judge in Israel!
He thought to build his Paradise
With tools that had been forged in Hell.

If, double-minded, lost to shame,
He dallied with such thoughts as these,
Then, when the disillusion came,
What icy fear his blood would freeze!
No washings now could cleanse that hand:
Too late to cancel his intent
When Heaven and Earth both seemed to brand
The guilty brow of him who went
In dark concealment of the night
To set in motion that great crime,
His name now writ in lurid light—
A by-word until latest time.
We see the clammy sweat of fear
Like that upon a dying brow,
And all the base ill-gotten gear
Seems to the sinner hateful now.
A hunted man, he knows not where
For him the way of safety lies;

A wild beast making for his lair
Might show such terror in his eyes.

"For him, of all men most forlorn,"
'Twas so the words of Jesus ran,
"Better he never had been born."
He lived to bear the name of man,
To show how low a man may fall,
In one man's life what worlds of woe
May lie concealed, and how through all
One thought of mortal sin may grow.
What hope can brighten on his way?
The flush of ardour on his face
Has faded to an ashen grey.
In days gone by, a child of grace,
Apostate now from good, farewell
For ever he has said to peace.
Some friends he had before he fell,
But now the desperate caprice
Of sin with every thought entwined
Has made his life a solitude.
No balm for him, no love to bind

The broken bonds of brotherhood !

No more for him the gracious smile

At which his heart had often leapt

When, childlike still and free from guile,

The secret fires of passion slept.

No more the blessèd comradeship

With men who showed in kindling eye

And thrilling voice and trembling lip,

How pure their love, their aims how high.

As when, with longing in their eyes

The first transgressors, driven forth,

Looked back on their lost Paradise,

Well knowing now what sin is worth,

So he, as by a flaming sword,

Was driven far, through all pursued

By love's reproach, more clearly heard

Amid that dreadful solitude.

The holy converse that had made

Upon the slope of Olivet

Its own retreat within the shade,

Was now embittered with regret.

Undone—undone !   To turn from this

Rich banquet of the purest joy,
And all the fabric of his bliss
To see one fatal hour destroy !
Before the priests he cast the bribe
Accursèd, and by blood defiled,
One moment stood to hear them gibe,
Then fled despairing to the wild.

The crime appears so devilish,
Transcending so the thought of sin
Maturing in a mortal wish,
That Judas with a cruel grin
From ancient canvas leers on us
As if he were not man but fiend,
And, with a fancy credulous,
We see the demon hardly screened
By features like to those of man,
As if the Hell from which he came
Itself devised the hideous plan,
And left it lurid with its flame.
But deep within the human soul
There lie the germs that may expand

In thought and feeling, till the whole
Is marred as with a burning brand;
Yet in the worst, a royal will
Can wrestle with the enemy,
And crush the rising growth of ill;
And such a human will had he.
The crime was human, and the tale
Belongs to this historic scene;
Ah, could we know, the time would fail
To tell what deeds like his have been!
To bear no cross, yet clutch the prize;
To worship nothing but success;
To look with hard unfeeling eyes
Upon the deeds that good men bless;
To turn religion to a trade;
To wear an outside cloke of zeal
Till all becomes a poor parade
To cheat the simple; and to feel
No tender reverence of heart—
Has history shown none of this?
No actors who have played their part,
And sealed it with a Judas kiss?

In cloud the wandering star had set:

On that horizon, once so clear,

A shapeless horror lingers yet.

Unhappy soul, gone mad with fear,

A castaway, forlorn, bereft

Of all that moves the life to good,

No shred of earthly comfort left,

Did no good spirit o'er him brood?

No hour of meek repentance come

Effectual and deep, though late?

The solemn oracles are dumb

That hold the secret of his fate.

The harvest past and he not saved—

Is that the ending of the tale?

What grace the hardy sinner craved

We know not, or with what avail;

Yet in our penury we glean

Some ears half-crushed by trampling feet,

Where busy groups of men have been,

And sift again the soilèd wheat.

We hear the holy sound of prayer*

---

* St. John xvii.

When all the men whom love had called
Were trusted to a Father's care.
One only love had failed to hold :
One craven would not bear his cross—
And here the sound is like a knell.
We ask if this was utter loss
For Time and Earth, and Heaven as well.
It seemed as if there feebly glowed
A smould'ring spark of good within :
Not hardened quite, the conscience-goad
Still drave him, maddened by his sin ;
And so from life he brake away,
As one who knew that life had now
No hope to lighten the dismay
That set that horror on his brow.
All lost for earth, no vista led
To sure achievement, and the dream
On which his earth-born hopes had fed
Was swept away with man's esteem.
So scared by what his hand had done,
Dishonoured and a fugitive,
There was no place beneath the sun

Where he could find the heart to live.

Inscrutable, mysterious grief !

We shudder at the dark despair

That did not dare to seek relief

In words of penitential prayer,

And at a climax of distress

So great that dreams of power and fame

Were now all changed to bitterness,

And death alone could hide his shame.

All lost it was for earth indeed !

In Hinnom where the constant fires

The heaps of outcast offal feed,

The mortal part of him expires,

But what of the immortal part ?—

The mind whose essence cannot die,

Which doth not perish but depart,

And once had set its aims so high.

What if an angel in the way

Should meet him as he flieth far,

With sword uplifted as to slay,

Yet hold his hand, since God doth bar

The way that leadeth down to death,

And fights against the man's despair
Until the heart he softeneth
And wins to penitence and prayer?

He hid from man, but not from God,
For man is blind, but God sees all,
And, though he bears a chastening rod,
He seeketh still the souls that fall.
The secret agency of pain
Has meanings deeper than we know.
The opiates that cloud the brain
Raise visions wild that come and go:
Through nature's heavings of distress,
Through fever heat and deadly chill,
Through days and nights of wretchedness
The soul benighted wanders still.
Then comes the crisis of his fate:
The eyes unclose, the brain is clear,
And watchers that like angels wait
Bend down, and whisper in his ear.
If such a change as that might be
Within the sphere of Nature's law,

A sadder, stranger history
We trace with a profounder awe.
There is a sickness of the soul
That passes through its fever fit;
The fell disease defies control,
And all who see despair of it.
And yet, despite delirious cries,
When all the fever rage is spent,
A soft expression in the eyes
May show, to their astonishment,
That some reserve of life within
Remains unconquered by disease,
And vital energy may win
By steady growth and slow degrees,
In that tremendous fight with death.
Through shame, through fear and penitence,
There struggles feebly back the faith
Long clouded by the mists of sense.
And angels, watching over men,
Raise cries of joy through all their host,
As when a brother comes again
Who wandered, and was almost lost.

The heat of the eternal fire
Consumes to utter nothingness
The evil things; but still aspire
The living forces.   That distress
That kills the sin, the soul may save.
We stand too near our life to see
The real worth of what we crave,
But death solves many a mystery.
If he who sinn'd deplores his sin,
Against him no resentment burns :
The worst that grace may surely win
Who strayed and, grieving much, returns.
Did this man turn ?   Ah, who can tell ?
Remorse he knew, and inward woe :
He knew the height from which he fell,
But did he Jesu's mercy know ?
He could recall the searching look
That sought the depths within his soul,
And hear the words of stern rebuke
Of Him who seemed to know the whole
In every follower of His—
" *There are the last among the first,**

" *And some, in yonder seats of bliss,*

" *Will shine, on earth esteemed the worst.*

But, even "last," to find a place

Somewhere, though very far away,

Within the shelter of His grace,

Safe there, although so gone astray—

Beneath the serious warning gleamed

Some light of hope to cheer him yet,

When he, of man so ill esteemed,

Should purge his soul with pure regret.

The merest fragments from the feast

Of holy promise now were more

Than all the world: the very least

Comes back with power unknown before.

Although he knew not yet the plan

Where righteousness and mercy meet,

" *No sin against the Son of Man* " *

Could drive the sinner from His feet.

If he to that one spar could cling,

When cast upon those waves of fear,

---

* St. Matt. xii. 32.

And feeling all that suffering,
To shore that spar might drift him near.

Again we glean in that great field,
So often trodden, sifting o'er
The grains of promise it may yield,
Though scant at best may be the store.
All rack'd with pain, the Saviour cried,
" *They know not, Father, what they do,*
" *Forgive them all."*   And when He died,
To find the words of pardon true
Became to more than one the sole
Remaining hope for life or death,
Till o'er the wounded spirit stole
That only peace that comforteth.
And doth the wisest truly know
What mean the deeds of youth or age,
Or how the sins take root and grow?
He marketh not the early stage
In which he dallied, half in play,
With fair enchantments of the sense
Until there came a fatal day

When he had lost his innocence.

Is one wrong turning to define

The place a soul shall occupy ?

Like one upon a steep decline

Who looks with terror in his eye

Upon the yawning gulf below,

Yet cannot stay his downward course,

Is it indeed determined so,

That, passing on from bad to worse,

The soul that, in life's little day,

Had somehow missed the heav'nward path

Can never find it now for aye,

But all capacities it hath

Shall only be consummated

To bear one long immortal pain ?

Among them all, the poor lost dead,

Will no kind Christ appear again ?

No strong and great Deliverer

Throw wide the long-closed prison-door

With news to make the dead hopes stir

From some far-off and happy shore ?

Is there a region anywhere

So sever'd from the realm of grace
That God Himself is powerless there,
Some foul usurper in His place?
Has Evil immortality?
Or is it but a slow disease
That wastes the powers, till Love sets free
The will enslaved, with words of peace?
What vital energies may move,
What more than human tenderness
To quicken spiritual love,
What angel forms may stoop to bless
We know not, for the narrow scope
Within whose limits we can see
Shows nothing clearly; but we hope
That He who, like a shoreless sea,
Has depths of love beyond our ken,
Will prove, although He waiteth long,
That he can sway the wills of men
Bewildered in the brakes of wrong.
And even now, the lifted veil
Of Inspiration has revealed *

* I. Cor. xv. 25.

What is the Power that must prevail.

The enemies of good shall yield

To His compulsion, Who must reign

Until His conquest be complete,

When Death and Sin and Grief and Pain

Are beaten down beneath His feet.

The realm of death itself is His,

For He has, entered it, and passed

Unscathed through its solemnities:

It owns its Conqueror at last.

Though now the air is thick with strife,

Eternal Love the sky will clear,

And in the deep abyss of life

Ingulf the elements of fear.

The purposes of God are sure:

With him the years are as a day;

Through storm and calm His plans mature,

Whilst we grow weary with delay.

We look upon the wrapping folds

Before the canvas is unfurled;

The fulness that His Being holds

G 2

To robe in light the breathing world,
To mould a purpose, or to make
The secret seeds of good expand,
We cannot know, till day shall break,
To show the workings of His hand.
We see not how the rebel will
Can ever change; but faith must stay
On Him who can Himself fulfil,
Though in His own diviner way.
Through all the ages long of Time
We see not mercy at the core
Of Retribution dogging crime :
We see the fact and nothing more.
For stern the lessons of the school,
And partial all we learn in youth,
We cannot see, behind the rule,
The heart and substance of the truth.
But God is not indeed Supreme
If everlasting sin can flout
The will that worketh to redeem.
Then God Himself is left in doubt,
And there remains a citadel

That Good is impotent to scale ;
Intrenched within the walls of Hell,
Iniquity doth still prevail.
The unbeliever on this blot
Has laid his finger with a sneer :
The sentence on the souls forgot—
" *Abandon hope who enter here* "—
He hints, is hardly quite a sign
That love is potent everywhere,
Or, if it be then love divine
Another dress than ours must wear.
And Faith finds here a stumbling block
To cast the feeble in the dust.
But on the everlasting Rock
We plant our stedfast feet, and trust ;
For love is mightier than all
Resistance of the alien will :
The strongest battlements shall fall
When He saith : " *I am God ; be still.*"
The sceptre of the universe
To Him belongs whose love is crowned
When all the warring hosts disperse,

And through His realm His praises sound.
The way is dark, the end is clear:
The storm is beating on the shore
But on the mountain tops appear
The glories that shall fade no more.

But ah, the meanwhile history
Through which one human soul must go!
Lo, drifting on a rock-bound sea
O'er which the gusts of Passion blow,
One drowning, catching at a straw,
Who sees outstretched a saving hand
That from the jaws of death can draw
The lost, and bring them safe to land!
Why burst the gale, why shipwreck came,
Why Nature rose in anarchy,
Why golden hopes die out in shame,
And wills created to be free
Can cast away their heritage,
Is utter mystery to us.
And how when storms have spent their rage,
The life can grow harmonious,

Our speculation asks in vain :

Philosophy gives little aid

To solve that mystery of pain :

There free enquiry shrinks afraid.

The poverty of our resource

Enfeebles hope ; and yet the Will

That guides all Nature's grander course,

Holds fast its changeless purpose still.

God willeth all men to be saved ! *

The love that feebly glowed on earth,

The purity it fondly craved,

He bringeth to a second birth.

In embers of the spent desire

Within the secret soul of man

There yet may glow with holy fire

The spark His breath alone can fan.

The promise stands : the discipline

That works the change we partly know.

The Mercy that destroys our sin

Though by the healing touch of woe,

* I. Timothy ii. 4.

We know as blessèd chastening,

And, though its methods are severe,

It softens to the souls that cling

To words of promise spoken here.

And if the film upon our eyes

Is not so thick but we can see

How griefs our evil things chastise

To teach us that great liberty

Of serving with a perfect heart

The only Uncreated Will—

And if, although the wound may smart,

No suffering of ours can chill

The love that all our life hath fed,

Why should we think that He will change

His mode of dealing with the dead?—

That not in mercy but revenge

His hand will strike?—that, changed indeed,

No Father but an iron Fate,

Like that of some dead heathen creed

Which deifies immortal Hate,

Will hold His purpose without end,

While souls that sinn'd, bereft of grace,

Without one motive to amend,
See only terror in His Face?
He changeth not: our mortal pain
He made His own: our misery
The Son that was without a stain
Embraced, and set our nature free.
And well worth while it were for all
To bear the pangs of suffering
If He who drank the bitter gall
Be owned at last as Lord and King.
Let woe be ours, so sin be slain:
Each soul its Cross must somehow bear;
If here we drag our lifelong chain,
It surely will be broken there.

Around one Sun the Worlds revolve;
We rest in God: to Him we leave
The questions that we cannot solve.
No human systems can bereave
The heart of this sure confidence,
That His resources can avail
To move the soul to penitence,

Though all our human methods fail.
So, if our questionings of doubt
Concerning this or that career
Remain unanswered, the devout
Will say, with mingled faith and fear:
" *With this we fain must be content—*
" *If, how and wheresoe'er it be,*
" *A man can soften and repent,*
" *A Heaven once lost he yet may see !*

Didymus.

THERE long has rested on his name
  A censure only partly just.
No servant truer to his trust,
Or one more lofty in his aim,
But at the last there fell on him
A blow that stupefied his sense :
He would not make a poor pretence
Of seeing when his sight was dim.
"I have not looked upon the Christ :
"I trust no other eyes," he said,
"They come not back, the sheeted dead;"
Nor witness of the rest sufficed.
He treated with a high disdain,
As one to whom the truth was more
Than all the tales that rumour bore,
The men who trifled with his pain.

Too scornful and too passionate !

Disdainfully his biting tongue

Denial like a weapon flung.

Such fervid doubt will alternate

With some reactionary chill.

The quick imagination plays

Till thought is lost in mere amaze,

Some strange enchantment on the will.

He failed, as other men have failed,

To hold his ground ; for hope deferr'd

Grew sick with fancies, till he heard

A voice that all his heart assailed.

Yet that disciple, with the rest,

Had once, without misgiving doubt,

With Him, the living Christ, set out

To live or die ; for which was best

He knew not yet, nor cared to ask.

His step was hopeful, strong, and free ;

If die he must he would not flee,

But had not counted on the task

So grevious to the mortal sense,

To walk by faith, to feel his way,

And, in the hour when hopes decay,
To rise above the influence
Of merely carnal love and grief.
Adown the valley of his woe
In pensive memory to go
As yet was all to him : belief
In One Unseen needs time to grow.
The cherished images that fill
The fancy, when bereaved, are still
Of earth, and in the tears that flow
All is not bitter; for the heart
Pours forth in grief its yearning love.
So Thomas mourned, as if to prove
How true affection claims its part
With all the past, though hope be dead.
To tell him he was not bereaved
But mock'd him—they were all deceived !
He pitied them as men that fed
Some fantasy of fond desire
On these delusive dreams, to stay
The pain that would not pass away ;
Such hopes would flicker and expire.

He dealt with them as men that rave,
Irreverent, that waste their breath,
And show a want of awe of death,
And desecrate a recent grave.

We trace a kind of parallel
Between the doubters, new and old.
Mere lookers on, outside the Fold,
They speak as if they loved Him well
Whom yet they cannot quite adore.
They reverence and they admire,
Declaring that His words of fire
Are living still, and ne'er before
Mankind had heard such noble speech:
And flowers they strew upon His grave.
Nay, that the world itself should crave
For such as He, and men should preach
And teach a doctrine so profound,
And celebrate His fame in rhyme—
They own it wholesome for the time.
It is a crying from the ground,
The sighing of a great desire

For man's ideal of the Good,
That would incarnate, if it could,
Mere phantom thoughts, and from the pyre
On which the Martyr sought His bed,
Behold Him like a phœnix rise,
And pass triumphant to the skies,
The Lord of all the quick and dead !

But cold concessions from outside
Offend us by their half assent.
When Unbelief was insolent
And scornfully the whole denied,
It had a soul of earnestness.
This dilettante kind of doubt
That reads the Gospel, but leaves out
The greater to allow the less,
And, with a show of reverence,
Bends to the spirit of the age,
Yet wears an air of patronage,
Is wanting in the finer sense
Of what this life of ours demands.
They differ here from him of old

Who, when he heard the tale they told,
Cried out to see the piercèd Hands.
His eyes the tears had made so dim
That through their mist he could not see.
"*A Living Christ could never be!*"
But if the proof were given him
That seemed so certain to the Ten,
The cloud would pass; the wondrous sight
Whose very thought was high delight
Would give him back his life again.

Then came to him the absent Lord
Who saw into his very soul,
And knew His servant's heart was whole,
And all his fealty restored.
In that great Presence standing now
The love that was of earth had passed:
For what He was he knew at last
The Master; for His noble brow
Was lit with glory, as of One
Still human, but whose royal mien
Transformed and dignified the scene,

A king of men, whose cause was won.
And he whose sluggish faith and slow
Had slumbered in an earthly tomb,
As one entranced in that poor room
Found all was changed. He could forego
The dream that clung so close to earth
To see Him now; and, deeply awed,
He owned Him for his Lord and God.

A God that through the gate of birth
Had come, and travelled by the road
Whose rugged surface jars the feet,
Who fainted in the sultry heat,
Whose tears for human griefs had flowed,
Who bowed His head at last to die—
His doubting servant owned all this,
Yet came with no familiar kiss,
As in the happy days gone by,
But now adoring cast him down
With words of faith that, coming late,
Through all the world's heart palpitate,
And constitute a sad renown

H

For one who, through the way of doubt
Attained the pinnacle of faith.
And still, though dead, he witnesseth!
If the Evangel had left out
That one confession, Christian Creeds
Were poorer now.   So Doubt may serve
To hearten feeble wills that swerve
When grief is strong and nature bleeds.

Gethsemane.

THE clouds have veiled the sky, as if to hide
  The actors in that tragedy,
And silently the ghostlike figures glide
Through deep'ning gloom from tree to tree.

A vague and half-expressed presentiment
Had been in all His words, of late,
That pointed on to some supreme event.
To watch with Him, to stand and wait,
If nothing else might be, to men so true
Was solace: as the Paschal feast,
Though served to them with bitter herbs of rue,
Had calmed and strengthened, ere it ceased.
His need of help was never more than then,
But none was ever so alone,
For Him the closest brotherhood of men

H 2

Could do so little, and His moan
Of spiritual pain, no human ear,
Though ever so intently strained,
Could gain perception quick enough to hear:
Deaf, blind, and helpless, love remained.

What mockery of love in life may be
He learnt, as in the days to come
His servants, torn with secret misery,
Would find the friendly voice grow dumb,
And miss discernment in the kindest eyes,
And so be driven in their need
To Him who suffered in this mortal guise
That He might all their secret read.
This human knowledge He was gaining now,
That men, from what He bore, might learn
The selfless love that can find room to grow,
Though often baulk'd of all return,
And with the gentle and forbearing tone
Of great compassion, can afford
To suffer human weakness, and condone
All love's offences with a word.

But ah, an agony more exquisite
Than even this was drawing near,
And down the vale of years, the thought of it
Is chill with rising mists of fear.
Entangled strangely in a maze of dread
He wandered, feeling for the clue;
He was as One some hand unseen had led
Through paths where hourly horror grew,
And yet, in all that wilderness of thought
One certain thing His faith could see,
That none must perish now whom Love had sought,
And, whatsoe'er the end might be,
He must complete His awful sacrifice.
Though blackness yawn'd beneath His feet,
Though Night was full of untold agonies,
Though Reason trembled in her seat,
He would not leave Him who had set Him there.
If all the tale of man's distress
Can reach Him surely on the wings of prayer,
The Father's love would stoop to bless
The well-beloved Son, as all night long
Beneath the stars He once had prayed,

And help had come to Him to make Him strong,
From Him on whom His faith was stayed.

So, in His mortal helplessness abased,
Began the solemn orison :
My soul is heavy, I am sore amazed—
Yea, even He, the sinless One,
Owned to the human weakness of despair—
My soul is sorrowful, He saith,
Father, the weight is more than I can bear :
It presseth even unto death.
We kneel in spirit at the fearful cry—
This bitter cup, if it might be,
I fain would let it pass, but how should I
Do aught but merely cling to Thee ?

What waves and storms across His troubled soul
That night swept wildly, none may dare
To picture even darkly, as they roll.
We see a part : His sunny hair
Is damp with dew : we see the sacred brow
So pure, majestical, but crowned

With drops of pain that soon like heart's blood flow,
And hide in darkness on the ground.
His high-strung frame, like some rare instrument
That thrills and throbs at every touch
In pulselike movement, shows a nature rent
With sorrow, none can know how much,
And life to Him is summ'd in suffering.
The memorable words He said
Three times, and still upon the ear they ring.
How many hearts since then have bled !
But never since the hour when Time was born
Has mortal known that mystic awe
That pressed on Him ; yet was He not forlorn—
His Father's will He owned His law.

No man was there whose pity might avail
The holy Sufferer for aid,
But weird, unearthly, rose the long-drawn wail
The winds were making in the glade.
The sound that to the purer heights above
The winds had carried on their wings
Was caught and treasured in the heart of Love.

Amid the holy communings
Of blessèd spirits rises the desire
Of loyalty, to succour One
So hard bested ; and from the eager choir,
In light as radiant as the sun,
There speedeth one good angel to uphold
The crush'd frail form of One thus laden sore
With all the burden of a grief untold,
That He may faint unhelp'd no more.

So all is ended : strength has come to Him.
When in the dark the torchlights glare,
They see a Man with eye no longer dim,
And for an instant they forbear
Before that royal glance and lofty mien.
But soon He puts His greatness by,
And yields Himself, and passes from the scene—
A King who reigns that He may die!

"This day thou shalt be with me in Paradise."

1.

THE malefactor, slowly dying,
  So long the law of man defying,
Now woke into a new contrition.
Full well he knew the great transition
From life to death his soul was nearing,
But light had come : the gloom was clearing.

2.

His comrade, long his anger nursing,
Now wild with rage brake forth in cursing,
As one, perhaps, who sinning longer,
Would vaunt himself in death the stronger,
Expend his breath in bitter railing,
And make no show of weak bewailing.

3.

But he, grown sick of all his sinning,
Retraced his life from the beginning,
And saw its meaning now more clearly.
If he had sinned and suffered dearly
He sought no veil for his transgression,
But made his meek though late confession.

4.

To Jesus on His Cross appealing
From Whom had come such swift revealing
Of what it is makes sin so fearful,
The dying slave, grown soft and tearful
Now felt the rush of pure emotion,
And prayed with passionate devotion.

5.

For him the time was gone for feigning,
But on the Cross his life's blood draining
The Saviour, seeking long, had found him:
The everlasting arms were round him.
" *To-day, in Paradise*," He told him,
A love more strong than death would hold him.

6.

So often, when the life is fading,
The conscience in its sore upbraiding
Is soothed, and through the solemn portal
There gleams the light of Life Immortal,
Since Jesus, though the heart be bleeding,
For all the lost is interceding.

7.

To see a man desist from scorning
To heed the voice of tender warning
That, even late, has found a hearing,
May prove to us that all the searing
Of sin upon the soul, one praying
May cleanse away, though long delaying.

8.

But though He pardons when entreated,
The work of grace is not completed,
For in that Paradise the knowing
The ways of God is always growing,
And, on the lesson ever poring,
The love grows only more adoring.

9.

The perfect man is not created
In one whose faith was so belated,
Except by much and patient learning.
In Paradise, the mortal yearning
Has changed its current of desiring,
And life is fed through pure aspiring.

The Rich Fool.

"This night thy soul shall be required of thee."

WHAT gain shall it be to a man to have won,
    Whilst crowds are onlooking, some coveted prize,
If, resting from toil, when the race has been run,
And the light has grown dim that dazzled his eyes,
The soul shall awake to discover too late
That all that is precious in life has been lost?
The end is so near, and the messengers wait
To tell him the river of death must be cross'd;
The message is urgent, and must be obeyed.
The apples of Sodom, so ruddy and fair,
Are as dust in his teeth—he sits there afraid;
He likes not the sound that he hears in the air.
The crush'd flowers of promise lie dead at his feet
The brief exultation, the shallow delight

Have passed like a dream ; he can hear his heart beat
To think of the things that may be in the night.
He sought not the treasure that waiteth on high—
The treasure no waste or decay can consume.
If once he desired it, the time has gone by ;
His barns are all filled, but he broodeth in gloom.
Ambition is empty, and honours are vain,
And he that was crowned as the king of the feast
Is lower than all ; there are shriekings of pain :
In the song of his life the music has ceased.
He is helpless indeed, so faint is his hold
On the things that he loved, and nothing remains
But waiting and fearing.   He bought and he sold,
And this is the end of his scheming and gains !
The vultures are round him before he is dead :
The man has been lost in the things that he had :
He knows that as soon as his spirit has fled
The faces will wreathe them in smiles that were sad.
They will talk to each other of what he was worth :
Each greedy expectant will count on his share ;
But as for the man—" *Dust to dust, earth to earth,*"
Is the empty lament that will rise on the air.

His pageant of life was a pitiful rôle;
And yet there is schooling for him as for all.
The eyes that were blind were the eyes of his soul,
And haply the scales of his blindness will fall
When, illusions all gone, his spirit has turned
To Him who makes life such a wonderful school.
The Master can wait till the lesson is learned—
Our hearts are so empty, and His is so full.

The Prophet Voices.

OF old, a voice from out the dark
A mystic expectation raised:
The patient prophets stedfast gazed,
And bade the listening world remark
When solemn rumours spread abroad,
And armies with their thundering tread
Strewed battle-fields with many dead,
Behind the scene, the march of God
As One who in mysterious ways,
When war has let its bloodhounds loose,
Turns all unto a higher use,
And makes the wicked hymn his praise.
The rays of light beneath the cloud
The lustre of His state proclaim,
And at the splendour of His name
Men bend, a rapt adoring crowd.

Each holy prophet was a seer,
The nations showed lit up in flame,
Before him the procession came,
And what he saw the world might hear.
But did he see ? The sceptic soul
That animates our modern life
Sees nothing but abortive strife—
At best, a race without a goal.
When men would build a stedfast bridge,
They cast across the chasm a line;
To straining eyes it seems so fine
That, as it goes from ledge to ledge,
They almost lose the sight of it ;
And some would ask if seers indeed
The hidden things of God can read,
And if their word is Holy Writ.
Well, let it pass—perhaps they dreamed—
A saner light is in our eyes !
Yet through these prophet-dreams arise
Such thoughts profound as men have deemed
Most precious in their waking hours.
So rapt in soul, if false their fire,

They kept alive the world's desire,
And reinforced with higher powers
The life that but for them had died.
'Twas work for heroes to perform,
To venture in amid the storm,
To breast the onset of the tide,
And, in the shrieking of the gale,
To hear a call in some dark hour
To wrestle with unrighteous power,
Strong in the cause that must prevail—
To play the man amid the strife,
And bear abroad a sov'reign charm
To cleanse the fierce from thoughts of harm,—
To give a larger scope to life—
To penetrate the dark Unknown,
And, in the might of holy faith,
To trample down the fear of death,
As men who know that none alone,
Unhelp'd and hopeless, live and die!
They bore a crest upon their helm
As knights and freemen of a realm
Whose King and Sceptre are on high!

The prophet voices that could still
The heathen clamour and the rage,
And carry on from age to age
Their witness of One holy Will
To which the wills of men must yield,
Drew all their superhuman might
From Him who, though He hides from sight,
To man His nature has revealed.

" I shall die alone."

(PASCAL.)

IN crowded halls ablaze with light
　　One sad-eyed brooding guest
Felt through the exquisite delight
　　A sense of strange unrest.
The melody to Pascal seemed
　　Too lulling in its sound,
Too sensuous : so men have dreamed
　　Of brows with laurel crowned,
And sought in Passion's fever'd joys
　　Their earthly Paradise,
And found their Heaven in the voice,
　　Or in the singer's eyes.
There Pleasure's fairest blossoms blow,
　　And yield their richest scent ;
But what is this that speaks in low

And sad presentiment?
Beneath the sweetness of the air
There sounds a lower tone—
"Although the world is all so fair,
Yet I shall die alone!"
Though gaily fingers touch the string,
And all is heedless glee,
Yet from the depths doth music bring
A weird solemnity.

To live alone were not so hard
For one who is a man,
For life itself is often marred
And hindered of its plan
By rude intrusion, and the noise
Of laughter in the ears
That fain would listen for the voice
Aye sounding through the years.
Or controversies loud and long,
So often empty sound,
Dispute the place with dance and song,
And each would hold its ground.

I think that I can live my life
   In my own fashion best :
I weary of the noise and strife :
   My spirit longs for rest.
A man may shun the moving crowd :
   Whatever risks he dares,
He waits not on their plaudit loud :
   He lives his life, not theirs.

Ah, yes, if units were we all,
   Each one himself a god,
We need not hear when brothers call,
   Or stretch our love abroad.
We do not need to turn for aid
   To battle with the wrong,
When hope has not begun to fade,
   And life in us is strong.
And, in the languid intervals
   Of utter listlessness,
When some mysterious shadow falls
   Of meaningless distress,
Perhaps we then would flee away

To some vast solitude,
And in the groves of silence stray
　Congenial to our mood.
But soon we find we cannot live
　Shut up in lonely thought:
The fancy is but fugitive:
　The mind was overwrought.
We want the faces that we know
　To cheer us with their light:
The cherished scenes of long ago
　Renew their old delight.
We turn to dear companionship
　In labour and in rest:
We would not willingly let slip
　The hand that love has pressed.

But if the weight of life grows less
　When friends beloved are nigh,
What then must be our loneliness
　When we shall come to die?
So dear and cherished, will they all
　Stand senseless at our side,

Nor answer to the fondest call,
    But in the darkness hide ?
Nay, may it rather be that we
    Have hidden from their eyes,
And, though they gaze and long to see,
    No glance of ours replies ?
In that our time of direst need
    Cast prone upon our bed,
Though words of comfort and Godspeed
    May tenderly be said,
Yet there is something in the scene
    That baffles love's desire :
A mystic veil has come between
    The lower love and higher.

Like some uncertain flick'ring lamp,
    Life burns but feebly now :
The hands are cold, the awful damp
    Of death is on the brow.
They see the slow and fitful breath :
    The spirit drags its chain :
They see how long he lingereth

Insensible to pain.
Ah, what is that obscurity
   Through which he tracks his way?
The night is long, and who shall see
   The breaking of the day?

There is an inner secret room
   To which the soul retires.
The vestibule is draped in gloom:
   Without are earth's desires—
Within—so changed from yesterday!—
   Can none go hand in hand.
Without, they kneel and weep and pray:
   Within, unseen may stand
The white-robed messengers of light;
   But none without that door
See aught but deepening shades of night
   Behind them and before.
We wait—we cannot enter in—
   Our love is far too weak.
Our breath has such a taint of sin
   We know not how to speak

In words to reach the ear of one
    So near and yet so far.
The words unsaid, the things undone
    Must go : the unseen bar
Between us now no hand can raise.
    No words of dear farewell,
Nor yet the long and meaning gaze
    The mutual love can tell.

But One there is who can be all
    That fellowship is here :
Within that room His soft footfall
    Might chase away the fear
If only through the walls of sense
    The spirit-sounds could stray.
The certainty of His defence
    Is more than we can say.
Perhaps the Gallic saint and sage
    Who listened to his soul
And, turning to life's closing page
    Where " Finis" sums the whole,
With half a truth was too content,

And; in that undertone,
Omitted something that was meant
 When he said—"*die alone.*"
It is not true: not quite alone
 They die who rest in Him.
We start to hear the dying moan,
 And, bending o'er life's brim,
We look with trouble in our eyes,
 But He who died is there,
And He will bid our brother rise:
 We leave him to His care.

The Comfortable Words.

1.

COME UNTO ME, AND I WILL GIVE YOU REST!
Along the wildly windswept rocky steep
The curling waves at last lie down to sleep;
There, where the storms have been the angriest,
On Nature's lips the kiss of peace is prest:
No foam of passion now is on the deep.
But Who is this that stills the fever'd leap
Of wild emotion in the troubled breast
Whose human yearning love, unsatisfied,
Has found in all no sweetness of repose?
From wanderings of vain desire we turn
To One with whom is no repulse, and hide
The blush of shame, the bitter tear that flows,
And He who pardons bids us cease to mourn.

2.

" *So God has loved the world !*" Our dim outlook

Is shadow'd, and we cannot see His Face :

Time has its terrors, and there traverse space

The crossing lines of pain we cannot brook.

From Nature turning to the Holy Book

Where all is written plainly, there we trace

From page to page, the stedfast growth of grace,

Till all can see what one dear Son forsook

To show the world how God in sacrifice

Held nothing back, but opened all His Heart,

And clasp'd us to it, giving us His best.

And then are soothed the low misgiving sighs :

When life grows sad, and fleeting joys depart,

We cling the closer to a Father's breast.

3.

A saying fit for all men to believe—

That Jesus Christ has come, and come to save

The very worst. No terror of the grave

Need darken faith, nor burden'd conscience heave

With pain, if but the sinner will receive

This truth in all its fulness. He who gave
His Son hath vanquished doubt; no heart can crave
A surer word of promise. Let us leave
Our vain devices to obtain relief,
And cast ourselves on Him. the Holy One.
Of all the sinful though we seem to stand
Branded, distinguished as the very chief,
He will not stay until His work is done,
And all are gathered at His own right hand.

4.

From perils that have thronged upon our way,
At last delivered ; for the peace attained
Our God be praised ! And yet we have not gained
The shelter of some tranquil landlock'd bay,
Where no ill thing can come, or friends betray.
Who of His rescued ones has not complained
Of sins besetting, feelings unrestrained
That seem to steal the purest hopes away ?
But if thou sin, oh, hast thou not the Christ ?
He knows thy weakness, and will advocate,

And not in vain, thy cause, and win His plea.

As on the day when He was sacrificed

Thy shame was His, He bears with thee the weight

Of all thy bonds, and yet will set thee free.

Consider the Lilies.

THE Lilies see—consider how they grow!
　　When Winter cast upon the sleeping Earth
Now all disrobed, her coverlet of snow,
It was as one who waiteth for a birth
Would shield the mother from the deadly cold;
There, safely shelter'd from the biting blast
The lilies lay.　So Nature doth enfold
Her treasures till the stormy winds are past.

What were they then?　No form or comeliness
Was theirs; no promise gave they of the grace
That now arrays them; none who saw could guess
The coming change, when o'er a pallid face
Would steal this roseate flush, this various tint
Of blended colour.　Groups of men passed by,
And saw, but thought not, as they came and went,

How that bare field the Spring would glorify.

The modest Earth was hiding from their sight

Her coming joy; but soon the bursting blade

Shot upward, and the genial warmth and light

Beamed on it, and around it daily played,

Till lo! with glory greater than of old

King Solomon in all his splendour wore,

Robed though he was in purple fringed with gold,

These orient lilies came, with all their store

Of secret glory flashing into light.

Their slumb'ring life had quicken'd in the breath

That maketh all souls live; and now the bright

Glad vision tells of Love that cherisheth

All that is hidden from us by the grave.

He Who thus decked the lilies, shall not He

Give back the lost for whom our spirits crave?

Yes, they will come, and when their forms we see

Radiant, immortal, fairer than before,

The lesson of the lilies will be read.

The earthly beauty will return, and more,

When they shall live again that once were dead.

K

The Journey to Samaria.

THE pastures sparkled still with dew
　　At early morn; but soon there grew
On meadow land and distant height,
Through gloom and grey of dawn, a light
That, with a glory all divine,
Stole o'er the face of Palestine.
Across the meadows richly grass'd
A group in friendly converse passed,
Afoot betimes, like men intent
On some far journey, while the scent
Diffused around from shrub and flower
Arose like incense, at the hour
That bids the sleeping world arise
To pay its morning sacrifice.

Their footfall fell by cottage eaves
Half hidden by the clinging leaves,
Through cornfields bare of garner'd grain,
·Then out into the open plain
Where, though they still were half asleep,
Life stirr'd among the drowsy sheep,
And lowing cattle called to men
To tell them day was come again,
And to an ineffectual light
Had paled the star, so lately bright,
That on the brow of Morn is set,
Although the sun's disc showed not yet.
But when that richer tract was cross'd,
The landscape all its verdure lost.
The signs of human life were few :
A dulness fell upon the view,
And presently from Nature's face
Had passed its bright ideal grace.
No leafy coverts cast their shade,
On no soft sward the sunlight played,
For plains unlovely, treeless, vast,
Without a shelter from the blast,

K 2

Stretched on before them, and no fair
Enchantment now was in the air.

But when Samaria drew near,
Life murmur'd softly in their ear.
Within a picturesque defile
The flowering shrubs began to smile.
Round trunks the wild clematis twined,
Its sprays toss'd gaily in the wind,
And here and there, the trickling rills
Into the valley from the hills
Brought freshness with them in their flow.
By banks where oleanders grow
Their pathway went, and through the trees
Came fitful movements of the breeze,
That hover'd like the soft caress
Of tender bashful lovingness.

Their step grew firmer : on they pressed,
Cheered by the hope of noontide rest,
While through the gate of every sense
Came some reviving influence.

But soon an open vast champaign
Of fertile undulating plain
Shows how the busy tiller's hand
Has set its mark upon the land.
The vineyards are in winter guise,
But wreaths of smoke from homesteads rise,
And, though the harvest long is o'er,
The farmyards bear their goodly store,
Telling of long industrious care
Ere yet the golden fields were bare.
The dusky olive copses cast
Their gloom upon them as they passed:
The almond groves, no longer green,
Now showed the struggling light between
Their naked limbs, whose fading tint
Grew ruddy in the passing glint
Of sunlight, as it dallied there;
And through the clear translucent air
Gleam upon gleam of radiance came
To fleck, as with a lambent flame,
Gaunt trees, and their more sombre hues
With richer colour to suffuse.

With welcome promise of repose
Mount Ebal and Gerizim rose
Fair in their sight: no need to tell
That now they near the ancient well
Dear to the heart of Israel.

At the Well of Samaria.

THERE, springing from a rocky bed,
And like a message from the dead,
They see the living water rise.
At Jacob's well, their musing eyes
Behold again the riven rock,
Their father and his thirsty flock,
And all the scenes of that old time.
None but the dwellers in a clime
Where fitfully the waters flow,
The blessings of the fountain know.
They rest awhile, then go to buy
Food to sustain them, lest they die.
But One is left, and yonder stone
A King hath chosen for His throne.
In want of rest, in want of food,

A man in utter solitude,
All travel-stained, in mean attire,
A peasant with no lordly sire,
Few would observe the regal air
In that meek Head that droopeth there.
His burning thirst he cannot slake,
As Tantalus upon the lake
Of ancient fable sought in vain
One drop to ease his constant pain.
But He would be a man indeed,
Our brother with us in our need,
Would understand our pangs of thirst,
And know our nature at its worst—
Take part in all with them that die,
And bear His Cross, and make no cry.

At last, a woman of the place,
A stranger, and of alien race,
Approached the well. Although she came
To succour that enfeebled frame,
Yet, only grave with household care,

She idly on her shoulder bare
Her empty pitcher. To restore
In Him the wasted strength—in her
New depths of secret thought to stir,
And all her void of heart to fill—
Little, as she came down the hill,
Deemed she that therefore she was there.
No voice prophetic in the air
Bade her prepare her soul to see
The truth of God that maketh free.

She saw a man of Jewish race,
But there was something in His face
That almost might conciliate
The bitter old Chaldæan hate.
Perhaps she feared the Hebrew pride,
And was inclined to turn aside,
Though womanlike, with look askance,
And curious meaning in her glance.
It was a gentle face, though sad,
And through His pride, if pride He had,

There gleamed a gracious tenderness.
Nay, there was that in His address
That showed His utter trust in her,
And, if she dallied, her demur
Betokened rather her surprise
To see His meek appealing eyes
Than callous hardness of the heart.
A Jew! the woman well might start
To see Him trusting her like this!
No curse had ever come amiss
To them of proud Jerusalem
Who feared to soil their garment's hem,
If such as she but passed them by.
Yet He—she asked in wonder why—
Dealt with her as a brother might.
He spoke as if He had the right,
As if her womanhood were more
Than all the signs her aspect wore
That she was one who nursed a feud—
As if He could discern the good
That lay beneath the alien crust,
And freely yield to it His trust.

And yet she listened doubtfully.

Give this man drink!   She knew that He

Was One who from defilement shrank—

How could He, when He stooped and drank,

Escape defilement?   For her hand

Was that of one the Jew had bann'd,

Renounced, accursed of God and man.

The very name Samaritan

Evoked a dull relentless hate

No lapse of time had power to sate ;

But Jesus taught the world the art

By trusting men to touch the heart.

He spake as if one common ground

Of pure humanity were found ;

And yet she puzzled at His word,

As if she had not rightly heard.

He had not wherewithal to draw :

Could He intend, despite the law,

To suffer her to give to Him,

To dip her vessel o'er the brim

And with the cooling drink allay

The thirst and fever of the way ?

What wonder if her hand delays ?
What wonder if she feels amaze ?
A woman of a mongrel creed
To help a Hebrew in his need !

Then He, in language mystical,
To that dark soul began to call.
Against her race His own might rave,
But He was One who came to save
The men on whom they fain would cry
For fire consuming from on high.
Of all the prophets He was first
To win with blessing the accurst,
And raise the sinner's drooping head.
This temper showed in what He said—
" *Didst thou but know Who speaks to thee,*
" *And all thy spirit's penury,*
" *Then thou wouldst ask of Me, and I*
" *Thy cravings all would satisfy.*
" *Lo, at this well the sons of men*
" *Come oft to drink, and thirst again,*

" *But from a deeper source I bring*

" *To thirsting souls, a living spring*

" *Whose waters mock not, nor run dry,*

" *And they who drink shall never die.*"

His speech was of a higher good

As yet but dimly understood ;

But now the scene had changed to her,

And she was the petitioner.

" Give me this water," was her cry,

" Instead of each day's poor supply."

Mere freedom from an irksome task

Were all the words appeared to ask,

Some hope of freedom from the toil

Of household care, the daily coil

Of meaner things, that gathers round

A life shut in by narrow bound,

Arose within her, but as yet

There was no passionate regret

For wasted hours : no voice within

Bade her bethink her of her sin :

And yet there was a dawning too,
Though dim, as dawn is, to her view,
Of what in life is loveliest.
A sense of trustfulness and rest
Unconsciously stole over her, .
And, as her thoughts grew tenderer,
The sweetness of the Stranger's voice
Subdued to holy calm the noise
Of restless oft-recurring care,
And fell upon the soul like prayer.
As in the Temple's shade, the life
That shelters from the outer strife
In that dim light gains some faint view
Of what it might be, born anew,
The soul that long had slept has stirr'd,
As when a loving voice is heard '
That calleth at the break of day
To bid the sleeper rise and pray.
Yet not at one swift sudden bound
Can any reach the depth profound
Of words that, glorious and divine,
Can stir the torpid blood like wine.

Dry questions of mere ritual
Stand to so many souls for all
That represents the great desire
To worship and adore. The fire
Of hot debate which they can feel
Is like the mimicry of zeal,
And all the wrangling of the schools
The hungry soul with husks befools.
The outside questions of the hour
Discuss'd with heat, can overpower
The urgent message to the soul
That seeks to lay its strong control
On thought and feeling and desire
Till dreams of earth grow purer, higher.
So she, to meet the fancied mood
Of One who no doubt understood
The controversy raging long,
And prove to Him that she was strong
In all the fence of argument,
Proposed, as one on truth intent,
To put to some decisive test
Which way of worship was the best.

But He, on no false issue led,
Refused that dreary path to tread.
The mention of her husband's name
O'ercast her argument with shame.
The matron's dignity and grace
That shelter'd in a pure embrace
Were gone from her: so long ago
Her womanhood had stoop'd so low!
Whence had He gained this power to scan
Her life, since life for her began?
Her quicken'd sense could ill endure
That glance of His, so heav'nly pure.
She knew, in that mysterious pain,
The real nature of her stain—
Nay, more than this, her every deed
Here was a prophet that could read.
The sin that, hidden in her breast,
So long had lain, was manifest.
She saw her very self at last
Adown the vista of the past:
Perhaps her life before her rose,
Its passion, and its false repose.

She saw again the barren years,
The brief delight, the long-dried tears,
The new-born hope, and then the pain
That told her she had loved in vain.
Each former wound had left its scar :
With self herself had been at war :
The echoes of her vain desires
Of passion, love, and jealousy
Came, like a wailing from the sea,
Where shipwreck'd hopes and projects drowned
Give tragic meaning to the sound.

'Twas strange that this mysterious
Chance interview should move her thus !
One hint at what her life had been
Brought other actors on the scene,
And ghosts, long-buried, came again,
And faces of forgotten men.
The soul that to accusing eyes
Is all laid bare, with new surprise
Discerns the heinousness of sin
At last, at last, and then begin

L

By methods that we cannot trace,
The workings of mysterious grace.
But over all her spirit's strife
There came a breath of purer life,
And, moved by stirrings of new love
That lifted her so far above
The sordid past, she called to her
Housemate, and friend, and villager,
To tell them all the wondrous tale,
And bid them the Messiah hail.

They came, the village patriarch
On whom the years had set their mark,
Wearing a look of grave surprise,
The women with their great brown eyes,
The swarthy men : all, half afraid,
The unaccustomed call obeyed.
The words she spake are left untold :
At first abashed, then growing bold,
Perhaps she sought her way to feel,
And they, who saw her new-born zeal,
Were smitten into reverence,

And saw in her the evidence
That found its way to every breast
Till they, with her, the Christ confess'd.
How much they knew, we cannot tell:
Their simple hearts before Him fell,
And, knowing Him, they knew the whole
Glad Gospel that redeems the soul.
They entered a compulsive school,
And they who know but that one rule,
To follow on where'er He leads,
Will find that what their nature needs
To round the sphere of life in bliss,
Is all consummated in this.

Sonnets on the Resurrection.*

I. NATURAL ANALOGIES.

THE chrysalis may cast his husk, and spring
    Into the glad pure air, exultingly,
As one that now has but begun to be—
Transfigured, beautiful, and on the wing
Find sweetness everywhere—a glorious thing
Instinct with life, emancipated, free
To range at large from flower to flower.   But we—
Is it a vain and fond imagining
That makes us dream we too shall cast aside
This mere integument of what we are?—
Shall clear the slumber from our heavy eyes,
And wake again, re-born, and, eager-eyed,
See well at last, where neither moon nor star
Shall look from out the dark of unknown skies?

---

*Suggested by passages in a treatise on the Resurrection by the Rev. S. Cox,
author of "Salvator Mundi."

II. THE ALTERNATVE OF DESPAIR.

Too vast the scale on which our life is built
If the Immortal prove an empty dream—
If virtues, graces, are not what they seem,
And men, in shrinking from the sense of guilt,
Are haunted only—if the night is filled
With phantom terrors, and, while daylight teems
With images of beauty, yet the gleams
Of glory are like players' tinsel, gilt
On some fantastic surface.   If the Christ
Was, like the rest, an evanescent shade
Who came and mocked us, never rose again,
And made a show of being sacrificed,
And all in vain—then, trifled with, betrayed,
Who are so wretched as the sons of men ?

III.   BATTLING IT OUT WITH DEATH.

We live this life of ours in eager haste,
Not recking how we spend ourselves, or how
The laws of life our labours disallow,
Our substance undergoing constant waste

By death fleet-footed from our birth-hour chased ;
And, as the furrows deepen on the brow,
The ebb of life is stronger than the flow.
Our very food is only waste replaced :
Men die, and other creatures must be born :
This sums the meaning of our present frame,
From first to last at deadly feud with death.
But there shall rise on man another morn,
When each immortal, changed and yet the same,
Shall live by other means than mortal breath.

IV. INSTINCT WITH LIFE.

The soul of life that animates the frame
The Stagirite distinguish'd from the rest
Of man ; but the mysterious interest
That centres in our being and our name
Would leave us with a riddle still unguess'd,
If this were all.   A life that puts to shame
These weak beginnings, and whose eager quest
Of things divine no alien voice shall blame,
The spirit longs for, and that life remains.

A keener insight, wider range of thought
Will mate with organs knowing not decay :
There living feeds the life, nor labour drains
The fount of being ; none sink over-wrought.
'Tis Life indeed—not keeping Death at bay.

V. THE LAST ENEMY DESTROYED.

To Him alone belongs the victory
Whose undisputed banner waves o'er all ;
And thou, O Death, though thou hast spread thy pall
On many dead, must doff thy crown ; for He
Has ta'en thy sceptre, and thy slaves are free.
Thy reign so long had lasted ! But thy thrall
Is broken now : low at His feet they fall
Who dreaded thee, and all their terrors flee.
Sin, with its poison'd sting, at last is slain ;
That horror, too, is gone : a better day
Is dawning on the world thou deemedst thine.
He has unclasp'd the cruel grip of pain :
The foes of good are worsted in the fray :
None question now the reign of Love Divine.

Christ and the Children.

1.

HE saw the children's silken tresses,
  He saw the mother's fond caresses:
He noted how the children smiling
Can charm the old with their beguiling.
And through the home the child-love stealing
Can quicken all the tides of feeling.

2.

The dull disciples, hardly knowning
The fount of love in Jesus flowing,
Rebuked the women for their boldness,
But they, unmoved by all this coldness,
Were still unto the Saviour pressing
To ask for even babes a blessing.

3.

With benediction on them looking,
No word He spake of stern rebuking,
But made the blessèd revelation,
That in the Kingdom of Salvation
The children often see the clearest,
And clear-eyed souls to Him are dearest.

4.

They see the Father's face, and alway
Their rippling laughter, like some sweet lay,
Comes up before Him, and He heareth,
Nor man nor angel interfereth,
And, when a mother's love beseecheth
'Tis He to her His secret teacheth.

5.

When scholars find their learning failing,
And wise men wisdom unavailing
To clear away the darkness falling
Upon their faith, their will enthralling,
Some pure young soul may be the angel
To bring them back a lost evangel.

6.

To men who think too much, Religion
Seems like an undiscover'd region,
Such questionings and doubts have risen.
They dwell within their narrow prison,
And still, the twilight dim preferring,
They do not trust the Guide unerring.

7.

Yet through the bars the pure light streaming
Will often set their spirits dreaming,
And, fresh from God, though immaturely,
The children seem to feel so purely
That from a spirit-fountain drinking,
They teach the better way of thinking.

8.

We see them, simple and confiding,
Within the Fold of Christ abiding :
There men that are the Kingdom seeking
Are taught to see the spirit speaking
Through which will grow the power of seeing
The hidden things beneath our being.

9.

In manhood, many things deceiving
May bound the range of our believing,
But childhood trusts the intuition
That tells us of our true position.
And, turning from the doubter, rather
Clings to the guidance of the Father.

10.

And so, despite the stern restriction
Imposed by men, His benediction
He gave to children to Him crying :
In life He blessed them, and in dying,
And every Christlike soul rejoices
To hear the happy childish voices.

Easter in the Sick Room.

WITH a blessèd welcoming
        Comes to all, the breath of spring.
Odours wafted on the breeze,
Singing birds among the trees,
Opening petals of the flowers
Sprinkled with refreshing showers—
All the bravery of dress
Robing Nature's loveliness,
Through the casement you may see
In your chamber though you be.
Draw the curtains; raise the blind:
On the window-seat reclined,
Thought can wander at its will,
While the quicken'd senses thrill.
Fleecy clouds their shadows throw:
Spirit-like, they come and go,

Hiding, gliding everywhere :
Witchery is in the air.

Nature, sleeping long, has now
Cast the veil from off her brow.
There is sweetness in her breath :
Full of life, she triumpheth,
Clad in graceful fair array,
And she bids us not delay
Welcome to her, nor to brood
In a dreary Winter mood
On the gloomy season past,
Now that Spring has come at last.
Open now the casement wide.
All things keep their Eastertide :
Morning, breaking into smiles,
Loneliness itself beguiles,
And the magic of her spell
Makes the sick folk almost well.
Ills may come to trouble joy,
Death the fullest life destroy :
Pain the tender heart may wring,

But, the Winter past, the Spring
In a way mysterious
Will most surely come to us.

So, in this beatitude
Musing in prophetic mood,
Souls uplifted in desire
Find the moving scene inspire
Expectations of a bliss
Vaster, more profound than this.
There are sweeter things than these
Borne upon the passing breeze.
Flowers there are that do not fade,
Light that need not seek the shade;
And the beauty of the earth
Fairer in its second birth,
Like a dream of pure delight
Rising from the lap of Night
Will renew upon the sense
More than Eden's innocence.
Death is but a sleep, and then
Comes the Eastertide again.

Sonnets.

TIMES OF TRANSFIGURATION.

HAPPY the moments when the foot can climb
    Up from the vale, to reach some Hermon height
Where forms celestial, robed in purest white,
Bend o'er us, and with their discourse sublime
Lift us above our thoughts of common time.
The ghostly fears that haunt the livelong night
Pass from us then, and standing in the light,
The soaring high aspirings of our prime
Are all outstript.   For ever we would stay
In that exalted mood, nor turn again
To servile tasks, and all the strivings mean
That drag to earth the glowing thoughts of men.
The light may fade, the scene grow cold and grey,
But that is ours for aye which once hath been.

ART AND NATURE.

THE artist loves the world, but not amiss :
    He makes no idol of it, but his eyes
Droop as it were in reverent surprise,
Like one beset by heavenly mysteries
Who feels, but cannot understand the bliss
That bathes his being, and by instinct tries
To clothe in life-like forms his dim surmise
Of some fair world yet lovelier than this.
He walks as one in an enchanted scene
Where graces flit about among the trees
Round which the fondling creepers cling and twine.
His is the wondrous borderland between
The sense and spirit-world, and there he sees
The skirts, half vanish'd, of some Form divine.

EARTHLY STRAINS.

THERE is too much of sweetness in the song :
    The overladen air is faint : there rise
Upon the sense fair dreams of Paradise,
Blisses of earth, but infinitely long ;

And sounds and scenes upon the fancy throng
Full of enchantment to the gazer's eyes,
Lulling the soul to sleep ; and the true prize
Is missed because dull Sense hath led us wrong.
The Kingdom of the Blessèd that we seek
Comes not by dreaming of the beautiful,
But through the girding of the soul to good,
The rebel flesh constraining by Christ's rule.
The pure in heart, the valiant, and the meek
Alone attain to that beatitude.

SHALL THERE BE NO MORE SEA ?

SHALL there be no more Sea ?   The lovely bride
    Whose glad embrace has kept Earth's youth so green,
Making each morning sweeter than yestreen—
Is she at last to perish from his side ?
Yea, shall there be nor ebb nor flow of tide ?
Shall " laughter of the waves " be no more seen ?
Nor Night reflect the face of Heaven serene ?
Nor far-off ships, by eager eyes descried,
Bring gladness to the weary hearts of men ?

M

Nor song of Ocean, with its low refrain,
Come like strayed music from another sphere ?

A Sea that knows not death will come again,
And in its song no boding notes of fear,
Or wail of grief, will fall upon the ear.

BODY AND MIND.

HOW quick, how subtle, and how delicate
       The movements of the body and the soul,
By which two natures blend into one whole !
The speech for which the thought is all too great
The face is almost able to translate :
The nerves, responsive to the mind's control,
Quick to perceive the harmonies that roll
In linkèd notes of music, palpitate
In ecstasy of joy.   The plastic hand,
A rare and perfect instrument, can mould
And shape the fleeting fancies of the brain
Till teeming thoughts to forms of sense expand ;
And kindling eyes grow bright as they behold
Some pictured scene upon the sunlit plain.

ON THE MOUNTAIN.

HERE, on the mountain top, the air is free:
  Gone are the sounds that break the calm repose
Of thought—the mingling voices, and the blows
Of craftsmen at their toil. The silver sea
Is seen afar, and faintly shrub and tree
Show yonder where the eddying streamlet flows.
Here we have left behind the earthly shows:
Here breathes an air of awe and mystery,
As if the Soul of all our life were near.
Far, far away may earthly passions rave,
As rave the storms upon the shingly beach:
Here all is calm: who cannot worship here
Is out of tune with Nature, like a slave
Whose torpid soul no solemn thing can reach.

THEY SHALL SEE GOD.

THY Being, Lord, is like a shoreless Sea:
  No storm-clouds break, no terror-speaking sound
Doth there the trembling voyager astound.
In the embrace of Thine immensity

All creature forms, all living things that be
In safety shelter. Man, a king discrowned—
His transient glory smitten to the ground—
Seeketh his being's sum and end in Thee.
Thou speakest not in thunder or the gale,
Not in the forest murmur, or the low
Soft mystic sighing of the evening breeze,
But One who is Thy Son hath come, with pale
Sad face, to show us Thee, and make us know
A love diviner than mere Nature sees.

THEY UNDERSTOOD NOT THAT SAYING.

THEY understood not, though He spake so plain:
    There was a kingly sorrow in His speech
That moved them strangely, making them beseech
He would no more ; for, as He spake, a pain
As of some discord in a joyous strain
Smote sharp upon the sense, and each to each
Looked wistfully, as if they could not reach
The meaning of that sorrowful refrain.
A suffering King ! The thought was far too high

For them to hold.   So aye start back in fear
The common herd, when the heroic soul
Conceives some purpose in a great career
Which may demand that he shall even die—
His eye intent upon a mystic goal.

AIMINGS AT COMMUNION.

F ULL many things to sweeten life are here,
    The social round, and poetry and song,
Glances of love, and in the festive throng
Is much that captivates the eye and ear—
The smile, the welcome, and the words of cheer.
Gay are the scenes of light, and love is strong,
And art, that ministers to all, is long.
But souls cry out for contact yet more near:
We need communion that shall reach the core
Of real being, and can freely share
The spirit-struggles that are out of sight,
Then on the wings of Meditation soar,
Anticipating regions yet more fair,
And scenes of joy suffused with holier light.

THE LAST HYMN.

THE song of faith that falls upon the ear
    Of them that die is full of sweetness. Then
The thought arises—" Nevermore again
" Shall voices that were pleasant to me here
" Discourse their music ! " Soon a rising tear
Gathers beneath those dying lids, and when
The last farewell is said, a true Amen
Requires a heart from loves of earth made clear,
Or faith so strong that, looking through the mist
Of death, it can discern a time when all
Who here have partner'd in life's wealth of good
Shall mingle in a greater festival,
And, with a sense of new beatitude,
Find that earth's ties last longer than they wist.

St. Mary Magdalene in the Garden.

SO sweet it is, although so strange,
　　To hear the tender tones again
That move the deepest heart of men !
And yet there is a sense of change,
For something that she cannot tell
Bids her in brooding thought prepare
To part, and in the trembling air
Are soft suggestions of farewell,
And through the quiv'ring leaves there stirs
A breath that is not of the earth,
A joy more full of awe than mirth.
Unto His Father and to hers
The Lord she loves will soon be gone—
Ah, let her make the most of this
The last of all her memories !
Yet will her faithful love live on.

In every place where He hath been
There will He seem to hover still,
And words of His her spirit thrill,
And faith discern Him, though unseen.
The branches of the Living Vine
For His dear sake her hands will tend
Till Earth and Heaven seem to blend,
And human souls become her shrine.
There, toiling on the dusty way,
She still will see the bleeding feet,
And each sad pilgrim will repeat
His bitter cross, from day to day.
Still will her love on errands run
To souls that are in evil case:
She knows so well His tender grace,
And she will bring them, one by one,
To know the sweetness of that life
Which all, by faith, may live in him,
Though seeing may be sometimes dim.
And then will Passion cease its strife,
And love survive without its pain,
For often that unchanging Friend

His messages of peace will send,
And loss give place to greater gain.
She slowly learnt the truth, but well:
When self within her wholly died
The love that death had purified
Grew, and the earthly idols fell.
So long on waves of anguish toss'd,
No more she sought him at the tomb:
Her wealth of love had wider room:
The Christ regained she never lost.

The Resurrection, when it came,
Transfigured all the former things:
For mortal love would fold its wings,
And life grows colourless and tame,
If, at the close, the silent grave
Ends all, and there shall never rise
The blessèd, with their tearless eyes,
To claim again the love they gave.
So He who came again to bless
One woman who had loved Him much,
Though He forbade her trembling touch,

Soothes mourners in their worst distress.

He tells us of a life so deep

That death is swallowed up in it,

And on its bosom infinite

Repose the souls that fell asleep.

He came again, and they will come

In all the freshness of their youth, ·

To tell us what life is in truth ;

And voices that so long were dumb

Will speak, but in the angel tongue.

When those that have been parted meet

Their tones will seem more purely sweet

Than those by pain so often wrung.

This Man continueth ever.*

1.

FROM age to age the Priests of old,
    In incense and in sacrifice
And rites of washings manifold,
Kept bright the light of waiting eyes,
But since they knew not Him to come,
And all their hope was dashed with fear,
In signs were asking, like the dumb,
That God would make His meaning clear.

2.

As each High Priest prolonged his course,
His eye grew dim, His vigour waned,
And men remarked his lessened force,
And how chill age his life's blood drained,

---

* Re-written.

Until one day, unclothed of strength,
Unrobed—no symbol on his breast—
He lay, a poor dead priest : at length
No more in death than all the rest.

3.

Then others came and passed away,
But handed on the priestly chain,
And priesthood struggled with decay,
And mystic rite with mortal pain,
Till One appeard and took His place
To celebrate a greater Rite,
In whom there dwelt a holier grace—
A man, and yet the world's true Light.

4.

And that High Priest will never die !
Himself both Priest and Lamb of God,
He drew the gaze of every eye
When He poured forth His own life's blood.
For ever He continueth,
And with Him all for whom He died,
For He who triumphed over death
Our hope of life has justified.

5.

The former priests in dumb-show all
Performed their sacrificial rite :
Each year a solemn interval
Withdrew them from the people's sight.
Mere mortal men, they came and went,
And none the purpose clearly saw
Of what the images had meant
In that preparatory Law.

6.

But He stands ever in our view,
The One atonement for our sin,
Our Sacrifice and High Priest too.
A Temple He has built within
Each soul that He has won from death.
No dumb-show now, but words of fire
For veilèd sign, clear light of faith,
And certain hope for long desire.

The Sons of Thunder.

I. St. JAMES THE GREAT.

[St. Clement of Alexandria relates concerning St. James's Martyrdom, that the prosecutor was so moved by witnessing his bold confession, that he declared himself a Christian on the spot. Accused and accuser were therefore hurried off together, and on the road the latter begged St. James to grant him his forgiveness; after a moment's hesitation, the Apostle kissed him, saying, "Peace be to thee!" and they were beheaded together.—*The Rev. F. Meyrick.*]

IT was the dream of poor Salome's pride

In that new order of His Kingly state

To see her sons in office by His side,

Distinguished by their place among the great.

But He was pitiful, and gently brake

To that proud mother sad and startling news.

Who not for glory, but for love's dear sake

Have left their all, may yet be called to choose

The way of pain, to prove their service true:

" *Yea, ye shall drink indeed my cup of woe—*

" *What if ye find it bitter as with rue ?*

" *Yourselves, and what ye ask, ye do not know.*"
But in the end they knew His meaning well:
The high heroic temper of their faith
Upheld them, and they bade a glad farewell
To golden hopes, and followed Him to death.

True Sons of Thunder, when the tempest rose,
Then did their eloquence that scathed like fire
Whate'er it touched, break forth upon their foes,
And startle with the splendour of its ire.
Yet not in conflict only did the Twain
Win for themselves their chaplet of renown :
Their love grew stronger, sanctified by pain,
And cast their high imaginations down.
Weaned from their childish visions of delight,
They bent their brows, prepared to bear the worst,
And found it easy, with the Cross in sight :
One suffered longest, and the other first.

The years were few the elder brother had
To bear his valiant witness for the truth
Which no vagary of the fancy clad

In false enchantment, as in dreaming youth.
The voice that, on the Sea of Galilee,
Had found the kindred feeling in his soul,
And made him toiler on a greater sea,
Still held him with a magical control.
In daily converse with the life unseen,
' A sweeter and more gracious temper grew :
His past, and all the things that once had been,
Faith taught his chasten'd sense to read anew.
His eye of fire grew soft in tenderness,
As if, through looking always on the Face
Of Him who died, His gracious piteousness
Had on the very features left its trace.
As when with groanings inarticulate,
Emotion pants for speech, and failing words,
In some recess of thought reverberate
The tones that touch our nature's finest chords
Of mystic voices, but so far away
That nothing passes through the gate of sense
But dim half-meanings of a melody
Whose subtle and unearthly influence
Has somehow sought and found a listening soul,

The compass of his being is enlarged.

As one who presses to a nobler goal,

With greater meaning now his life is charged.

His soaring aims have ta'en a wider range:

There is a look of Heaven in His eye

As if His purpose never now can change,

And Christ is All, to live for Him or die.

So fell that mystic music on his ear:

Sufficient for the day the daily toil,

But daylight passes, and the end draws near.

The dust of earth his naked feet might soil,

And subtle inward sin pollute his thought;

But there was cleansing: He who on the Mount

Had changed the nature of the men He taught

Still bathes the soul in waters from His fount.

" *Yea, ye shall drink,*" the Master once had said,

And now, but changed in tone, the promise came,

Not sadly, like a message from the dead,

But with a voice of power that owned the claim

This ardent soul had urged, that he might stand

The closest, when the hour of danger neared:

N

Though all had perish'd that ambition plann'd,
This hope, transfigured, was the more endeared.

The scene is changed: no honours tempt him on:
Who follows Christ must put to pain and grief
His selfish will: the Cross precedes the Throne,
Yet will the servant stand beside the Chief.
No shouts exulting and no ringing cheer
Of warring men proclaim that victory
Is close at hand; but ever in his ear
There sound the sad appeals of Calvary.
And as, in battle, madden'd by his grief,
Some hapless soldier casts himself away,
And death, the one effectual relief,
Embraces in the thickest of the fray—
So, driven on, wherever danger lies
This soldier of the Cross elects to stand,
And, where the fight is fiercest, only sighs
To hear One Voice more clearly in command.

But there are watchings, when the air is still
And sickly with some heavy influence,
As if a dim presentiment of ill

Had warned the spirit through the startled sense.

All danger lies not in the scene without:

There is the proud revolting will, the sin

That so besets the best, the restless doubt:

The foes that are the worst are those within.

Alas! so slowly Self consents to die!

Revenge is sweet: to suffer and forgive,

And to be wronged, yet pass it calmly by—

This, to the proud, high-souled, and sensitive,

Remains the critical and final test,

And failure here, in some unwatchful hour,

Has been the subtle peril of the best:

The flesh is weak, but grace will give him power.

So when there came the crisis of his fate,

Within the very shadow of the grave,

How love can quell the persecutor's hate

One other proof the dying martyr gave.

For, standing at proud Herod's judgment seat,

He showed that greater mastery of grace

That softens wrath, and makes the bitter sweet;

And when they saw the patience in his face,

And heard him say that Christ was more than all

The world to them who own Him sovereign Lord,
And that the recreant from His gracious call
Who shrank and shudder'd at the threatened sword
Were base indeed—the whole assembly thrilled
With admiration, and a solemn awe
Possessed them, and the savage shouts were stilled;
For here was one who owned a higher law.

But as they led him to his martyrdom
A strange thing chanced; for now he saw, in tears,
The man who was his late accuser come,
Protesting that through all the coming years
He could not know one hour of true-heart peace;
Then, growing bolder, though with trembling breath,
And clinging to the doomed Apostle's knees,
He prayed his pardon, and avowed his faith.
" *Could he forgive ?*"   He looked, and softly mused,
Bethought him of the lost that love must seek,
Then touched with tenderness that spirit bruised,
Spake peace, and stoop'd and kissed his cheek.
Together they confessed One Christ, One Lord,
Together then their dying witness sealed,

Together bent their neck beneath the sword :
But death has balm, soon all their wounds were healed.

So near in heart this proud fierce man had grown
To Him, the gentle Master, who had passed
Through keener pain than his, to reach His Throne,
Yet, ere He went, a look forgiving cast
On one long wander'd from His Father's fold,
Who saw the pity in His gracious eyes,
And turned to Him, and gladdened to be told
That he should see Him in His Paradise.
The young disciple's sanguine eye had seen
The promised glories of Messiah's reign.
The sky, once black with storms, had grown serene,
And there, outspreading wide upon the plain,
A host with banners floating in the air.
Or now the scene had changed. The Prince of Peace
With them who served would all His honours share,
And then the wrongs, the ills of life, would cease.
So soon that visionary scene had fled !
He saw the stain upon a bleeding heart :
He saw the drooping of the Sacred Head,

Yet, fired with purer zeal, the closer press'd
To One whose royalty seemed greater now,
Since He abideth ever who was slain.
He saw the glory round the thorn-crowned brow,
And panted still to follow in His train,
Attracted most by that undying love
Which prayed the Father to forgive His foes.

The days are dark, but in yon sky above
The clouds are breaking, and the glory grows :
The voice that calls him bids him gather in
One other soul.　They climb the rugged steep,
And brothers now, soon pass beyond the din
To where the Lord doth give His loved ones sleep,
Beyond the cries, beyond the mocking scorn.
Their union Jesu's love had made so sure
So die the dreams of earth, and so are born
The visions of a glory yet more pure.

II.　St. JOHN.

The links of sweetness in the common life
Of Christ's disciples, subtle, tender, sad,

We can discern beyond the scenes of strife
That scare the sense. For One had made them glad
With joy ineffable: it reached so deep
That there were no reserves of feeling now.
In tears they sowed, but by-and-by would reap
Their harvest, though as yet they knew not how.
An insight sensitive and delicate
So passed from one into the other's soul
That they were one: they could not separate
The elements that made that perfect whole.
Their friendship had been fondled into strength
By all that proves men, and through trial grew
That nobler form of friendship which at length
Showed that their Lord had fashioned it anew.
For self died out of it, and each friend passed
Into the other's life. To climb alone
To glory, or alone to bear the blast
Of persecution, was a thing unknown
To their new way of looking upon life.
So Peter bore his brother on his heart:
" Ah, would he suffer by the cruel knife ?
"And which true brother would the first depart ?"

He cried—" *Dear Lord, and what shall this man do ?"*
Yet shrank perhaps, and wished the words unsaid,
Such terror might be forced upon his view.
" *Nay, what is that to thee ?   If, long delayed,*
" *I bid him tarry till I come again,*
" *Let thine endeavour be to follow Me.*
" *Be thou content with that, nor ask Me when,*
" *Or where, or how, thy brother's end shall be."*

The best belovèd had to tarry long,
To see his comrades falling, one by one,
To stand a lonely man, amid a throng
Who marr'd the work of good in faith begun—
To pine, a captive on a rocky isle,
The ocean round him, where he could not hear
One kindly human voice that might beguile
His desolation with its words of cheer—
And, when restored to action, with dismay
To see the growth of error in the Church,
The pride of intellect, and the decay,
Through eager too irreverent research,
Of simple faith in some, and in the best

Too much of the ambition of the sage ;

To toil and still to toil, and long for rest,

And yet be kept expectant in an age

No longer glorious with the sunrise glow

Of holy love and self-consuming zeal—

His strong and tender nature lived to know

All this.   He could have better borne the steel

That sought his life ; but patiently he stood,

Though danger loomed, and storms were in the skies.

He bore the pain of seeing doctrines crude

Polluting the pure well of truth,—surmise

For faith,—a wisdom that was not of God

Diffusing vaguely a dissolving view

That, ever changing, seemed to spread abroad

A visionary semblance of the true.

The future that the Master would not tell

Has now receded to the past.   The mind

Of that disciple, like a sentinel,

Kept still its watch, to either fate resigned,

To challenge error, and defend his post.

He pointed to the Star whose silver light

Reclaims the traveller when almost lost,
Its liquid radiance flowing on the way
By which belated travellers may find
The home they long for, though gone far astray—
The home for which, despairing, they have pined.

And other men he stationed in the dark
To stand as angels with their pure white wings,
To guard the mysteries within the Ark,
And sometimes seize the harp, and touch the strings,
To wake the heart of all the Church to praise.
There, hardly veiled, he saw behind the screen
An awful Presence and a searching gaze,
And warned them aye to keep the soul so clean,
And fill the years so full of fruits of good
That they might stand accepted in the day
When all the dark things shall be understood.
Though, like a scroll, the earth shall pass away,
The deeds are living, and will reappear,
And things forgotten start into the light
With aspect menacing—so warned the seer.
His message to the Churches, read aright,

Is like a legacy to every age.

The man who lay upon the Saviour's breast

Has left it for us: as we turn the page,

We see what foes the earthly Church infest.

We ask ourselves if even such as we

May cleanse our robes from all their stains of sin,—

If these dull eyes may yet the glory see,

And, from the outer darkness, enter in.

To him the earth was eloquent with speech:

The roll of thunder, and the flashing fire,

The angry billows breaking on the beach

Shrieked notes of discord through his wondrous lyre.

But all that is most sweet and musical

And thrilling to the sense in mortal song

When consecrated to the Lord of All,

He heard repeated in the angel tongue.

Like to "the many waters" falls upon his ear

The voice of Him who holdeth in His hand

The stars of light: across the glassy sea

On yonder shore the white-robed harpers stand.

And in his vision rises through the mist

A world where all the tears are wiped away,
A city fair with pearl and amethyst,
Where purest robes the citizens array.
There evil vainly struggles with its fate:
At last eternal voices sound its knell,
Good only lives, and love has vanquish'd hate,
And in its deep have perished Death and Hell.
But o'er the mystic scene there sweeps an air
That has a breath of sweetness, as of earth:
The earth that was has gone, and yet more fair
A new glad life is hasting to the birth.
As from a lyre hung high to catch the breeze,
That yields its sweetness to the wooing air,
The notes of gladness in the strain increase:
The changeful melody subsides in prayer.

His twilight lingered, as the evening glow
Fades by gradations that no eye can trace,
Yet dies at last, and Night, with footstep slow
And softly stealing, shadows every face,
But when or where his spirit passed away—
If they who loved him gathered round his bed,

Upheld his soul, and, at his close of day,
Sang softly masses for the happy dead—
All this we know not; but we know full well
His holy fervour, in the waning light
When night was coming, ere the curtain fell.
His strength was broken, but his eye was bright,
As he discoursed of love, his only theme.
The foaming torrent of his eloquence
Had now subsided to a gentler stream :
The nearer to the end, the more intense
His ardent gaze upon the coming bliss
Where God no more doth cover up His face,
But all shall see Him truly as He is.
And, musing on this mystery of grace,
There brake from him the passionate desire—
"O come, Lord Jesu, let there be an end !"
The guest belov'd was called to come up higher—
Again were joined the Master and the friend.

A martyr some have called him—not "in deed"
But yet "in will." And who can better claim
Than the belov'd disciple, that great meed—

Who, knowing not the martyr's public shame,
Was martyr'd all his lifelong, suffering
Such intermingling elements of grief
To nature, and to stedfast faith, as wring
The heart too noble to seek base relief ?
Each day full many an aching heart endures
A martyrdom like this.   The growing pain
That vibrates on through life, death only cures.
Till Christ shall come, such martyrs will remain !

Commemoration in the Eucharist.

WHEN within the hallowed shade
    Of the consecrated fane
They who knelt with us and prayed
Come about our hearts again,
Then is unity restored :
Choirs of happy spirits sing
" Holy, Holy," to the Lord,
Joining in our communing.
In the very arms of death
Clinging to the blessèd Cross,
They divined the power of faith
And the gain that comes through loss.
They who seemed to fall asleep
From the world of shadows passed :
Now they live with God, and keep

Watch until we meet at last.
And the Church is waiting too,
Till the Sacraments give place
To a vision yet more true
Of the fellowship of grace.
Here there is a trysting-place
Where may souls long sever'd meet,
All the cherish'd past retrace,
And their purest vows repeat.
Earthly passion breathes not here,
But the air of Paradise
Is about us, and the dear
Look of love in tender eyes
Beams upon us from above,
Till the beating heart is stilled :
For the prophecy of love
Cannot be on earth fulfilled.

As of old, at Heaven's gate
One poor dreamer seemed to be,
When the Church doth celebrate
The Eternal Mystery,

Then do Earth and Heaven meet.

Though upon the mystic stair

We can see no angel feet,

Holy thoughts are in the air :

Cherubim and seraphim

And the spirits of the blest

Our Redeemer's glory hymn

In a greater Eucharist.

Blessèd souls from sin released

Mingle with their earthly kin

In the pauses of the Feast,

Where the spectral form of sin

Still may scare the earthly guest,

But the mystic Holy Rood

Lays the mortal fear to rest

With its mightier power of good.

We shall wander with them yet

In a world more fair than this,

All our passion of regret

Lost in fulness of that bliss.

Still the Master entereth

Through the closèd doors of sense,

And sustains the failing faith,
Languishing through long suspense.
And to-day, around His board
Others whom we cannot see
Broken bread and life outpoured
Take, though otherwise than we.

The Cross of Riches.

———

HE said it: The rich, in the Kingdom of grace,
  Where nothing remains but one standard of right,
Must yield to the poor their preeminent place:
The glory will fade that on earth was so bright.
This will happen to some, in the satire of fate,
Who sat at their feasts in their purple attire
While Lazarus, covered with sores at the gate,
Has attained to a bliss that mocks their desire.
Yet some of the great ones, more noble in aim,
Who sifted the gold of pure love from the dross,
Too humble in heart to put forward their claim,
Will avow that their wealth was their heaviest cross.
Though their coffers be full, the humble in mind,
Whatever their outer estate, will be blest:
God giveth us all for the sake of mankind,

And they are the richest who love men the best
And loving, around can everywhere see
Some image of Christ.   They remember Who said—
" The poor ye have succour'd : ye did it to Me :
" Me sick ye have tended, Me hungry have fed."
One day with the Lord of the feast they will meet
Who purchased them all at an infinite cost,
To find that the love they cast down at His feet
Is the one thing of all He treasures the most.
The noble and rich that He welcomes are they
Who gave what they had, if not silver or gold,
Yet the wealth of pure love that cannot decay :
He will not forget when His jewels are told.

Memorial Flowers.

1.

PLANT on my grave no summer rose
 That sheds its fragrant leaves and dies—
No flower that for a moment blows,
Then droops, and fades, and prostrate lies.

2.

Too sad a mimicry of death
By fleeting lives like these is given
Which pale their hues, and yield their breath
Without a hope, like ours, of Heaven.

3.

They live and bloom and pass away :
Their fragrance lingers on the sense,
For, beautiful in their decay,
No stain has marr'd their innocence.

4.

But never on their life arose
The hope that fills our own with light;
No soul has sunk to its repose :
It was not joy that made them bright.

5.

Each one a lovely thought of God,
Unconsciously they live and smile:
Fast rooted to their native sod,
They flourish for a little while.

6.

Unmeet they are to symbolise
This troubled, tangled life of ours,
Where laughter alternates with sighs :
They know no tears but summer showers.

7.

They never either toiled or spun
To clothe them in their fair array:
No thought of earthly works undone
Afflicts them as they pass away.

8.

The lily droops its graceful head,
But never felt the flush of shame:
To it upon its peaceful bed
No haunting terrors ever came.

9.

And yet the flowers may be a sign,
Though only by a mocking show,
Of life immortal and divine,
As changeful seasons come and go.

10.

For though they die and live no more,
They drop their seeds, and in the spring
All nature, smiling as before,
With happy life is murmuring.

11.

But ah, the life is not the same !
Unbroken being is not theirs:
A mere successor to a name,
Each flower its lonely beauty wears.

12.

And some would say this sums the case
Of us who masque in life's disguise :
The unit merges in the race :
The line has gaps, but never dies.

13.

Our thoughts take root in other lives :
The air of eld we seem to breathe.
The race, if not the man, survives :
Some legacy doth each bequeath.

14.

And this is all for which we live !
Death sounds at last the knell of hope :
The soul that was so sensitive
No life shall know of larger scope !

15.

Alas ! shall none live on his life
Beyond this crumbling house of clay ?
No great Commander crown the strife ?
No golden dawn lead on to day ?

16.

Is this to be our mournful creed ?
Our being check'd in mid career ?
Each soul that dies, a wither'd seed ?
The only Life Immortal, *here ?*

17.

This life a cheat and satire all ?
Prophetic voices but a breath ?
Shall none the wanderer recall
From straying in the Vale of Death ?

18.

If men abjure their heritage
It is but jargon to repeat
Their vain eulogium of the age—
The dead mere dust beneath their feet.

19.

In incoherent fragments then
The ages run their aimless course :
The actors are not living men,
But playthings of a mindless force.

20.

Our life goes out in barrenness:
For us, who have so much to bear,
No Helper in our sore distress,
No future outlook but despair!

21.

Is that the Gospel of the age?
Shall men, immortal in desire,
Search Nature on from page to page,
And find in all no teaching higher?

22.

Ah, well, with deadly nightshade then
Fill up the spaces in the ground,
If never shall the lost again
By love that waiteth long be found.

23.

No farther-world, no Paradise,
No depth of clear translucent air
Through which the strong immortal eyes
Shall see, undazzled by the glare?

24.

No Father's House ? No rest of God,
No safe and sure retreat, where they
Whose relics lie beneath the sod
In perfect rest the past survey ?

25.

No compensation for our grief ?
And no completion to the love
That, finding earthly life too brief,
Had centred all its hopes above ?

26.

Mere words ! ten thousand beating hearts
Are panting for the life to come,
And every spirit that departs
Is like an exile going home.

27.

The Life was manifest in Time—
The life in which all spirits live—
To tell us of a genial clime
Where no delight is fugitive.

28.

It is but dying out of death
When He shall come to set us free :
A little while there tarrieth
The hour of true felicity.

29.

If faith would deck a brother's grave,
Then choose the flowers that do not fade :
The good, the gentle, and the brave
Have found the light beyond the shade.

30.

We toilers on the earth may tread
Amid the shadows doubtfully,
But they whom now we call the dead
Know how the vain illusions flee.

31.

To mortal eyes futurity
Is dark ; we dread the distant roar
Of storms upon an unknown sea :
They stand in safety on the shore.

32.

They make our stream of life run pure:
Though dead, they speak to us, and say
Some words to keep our footing sure
When stumbling blindly on our way.

33.

Our parted rills of life will yet
Be reunited in one stream,
And all the passionate regret
Fade like an unsubstantial dream.

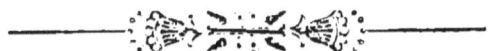

The Agony.

1.

THERE, beneath the olive trees,
    As within a sacred grove,
Kneeling low upon His knees,
Pours He out His heart of love.

2.

Three times o'er His anguish'd cry
Rises through the list'ning air:
Nothing but the night-wind's sigh
Breathes responsive to His prayer.

3.

Weary, worn, the watching Three,
Keeping guard beside their Chief
In His hour of Agony,
Sleep the sleep of utter grief.

4.

Nerveless now, distracted, sore
With the anguish of the day,
Nature can endure no more—
Let them sleep while yet they may!

5.

But the cry went not in vain:
In His soul the answer came—
" Welcome all the mystic pain,
" Welcome sorrow, welcome shame."

6.

" Let me drain this cup of woe
" If it be My Father's will:
" Let Thy loving purpose grow—
" I will suffer and be still."

7.

So, through hours of weary length
Men who suffer with their Head
Turn to Him, and gather strength
From the words of faith He said.

Sonnets.

THE MYSTERY OF PAIN.

THE pang of pain strikes deep, and quivering
    And sore amazed, we ask the reason why
He who looks on from out His place on high
Could suffer this one special evil thing
To touch us to the quick. We feel the sting
As if Himself had stung us, and we cry—
" Is there no God ? or doth He pass us by
" As One who heedeth not our suffering ? "
We ask for any other pain than this
That searches us; and yet can we forget
How One who suffered never once complained
Of hardness in the task His Father set,
But, lest the world some greater thing should miss,
Unto its dregs His bitter potion drained ?

FELLOWSHIP IN HIS SUFFERINGS.

TO be His fellow! What could Heaven give
    More fit to raise us from our lowliness
Than when He gave us His own Cross to press
Close to our heart?   He was so sensitive
That, when a woman who could hardly live
Through the protracted years of her distress
Touched but His robe, He felt the faint impress,
And turned to her, but only to forgive.
Such was His quick response to every touch
Of anguish in Himself: He could not hide
The marks that showed the pressure of His Cross.
By searching pain His sinless soul was tried,
And most, the pain of those who love so much
That if love triumph not, all life seems loss.

THE LAW OF LIBERTY.

THE rule of man is apt to be austere,
    Unsoftened by the touch of charity,
When stern unbending law can only see
That men are creatures strongly swayed by fear.

P

But that one Rule that makes obedience dear
Has found a better way, by which the free
Consent of man is won through clemency.
The heart's revoltings do not interfere
With law, when law gives speech to secret love.
Man's nature, overmastered by desire,
Seeks to break through its bonds of helplessness :
Athirst for good, it seeketh heights above
Its mean attainment, and so presseth higher,
Seeing the Ruler's hand upraised to bless.

"HE HEALED THEM ALL."

HEALER and Sufferer, He learnt to heal
      By bearing with us what we have to bear.
He could discern the thoughts of dark despair
That sadden men when sickly fancies steal
Around the couch, and, with a heart to feel
For hidden griefs, He laid His soft touch there
With quicken'd insight, and a tender care
That needed nothing but the mute appeal
Of suffering, to guide His sensitive

And sympathetic skill. The wither'd limb,
The deaf, the fever-stricken, and the blind—
He healed them all! He bade the dying live:
The sight of pain was misery to Him—
Its cause and cure the Friend of man divined.

WHAT LACK I YET?

*W*HAT *lack I yet?* The Ruler satisfied
    With the mere form of an ideal good,
And bounded in his scheme of rectitude,
Asks in the triumph of his virtue's pride,
Not knowing what within the soul may hide
Unknown and unsuspected, or how crude
Would show his goodness if he only could
See as He sees who standeth by His side.
He lacketh love, and that is everything:
Alms he could give, nor count his gains the fewer,
But—to give *all!* He learns from that hard test
To know himself, and see how there may cling
About a heart that seemed to be so pure
Base things of earth—then turns in much unrest.

HE LED HIM ASIDE FROM THE MULTITUDE.

NOT in the throng of men, whose restlessness
 Disturbs the calm of thought, the Lord doth give
Sure token of His presence.   Fugitive
And often vanishing amid the stress
Of common things, the thoughts that Godward press
Pass swiftly out of sight ; and yet they live
Within the spirit's call.   The sensitive
And subtle tremour of the soul's distress
Returns, and chiefly then when led aside
To the sick chamber's stillness, or the place
Of secret oratory, where no eye
But His can see us—scenes so beautified
By visitings of His sustaining grace
That life revives, and mean affections die.

Emmaus.

I. THE WALK TO EMMAUS.

WHY should they dally longer now
　　In streets that thronged, with none to share
Their anxious thoughts of brooding care?
The scene had changed, they knew not how.
An evil cloud upon the Feast
That year had fallen: dull despair
Was hanging in the heavy air,
While frantic rage, in scribe and priest,
Looked out from wild and bloodshot eyes.
Now all was over: it was time
To leave the place where coward crime
Befouled the scene of sacrifice.

Their friendship was a sacred thing,
A converse fervent and sincere,

Held back by no reserve of fear,

That sought the closest communing.

It was a placid rural scene,

At that bright season loveliest:

The sun was sinking to the west,

And Earth had spread her carpet green.

The dreamy sweetness of the hour,

The hum and movement of the bees

Amid the fragrant almond trees,

Then in their lavish wealth of flower,

The intermingling light and shade,

The whir of insects on the wing,

The sounds as if of whispering,

As in the leaves the soft wind played—

All this might well the spirit woo

To mere luxurious repose ;

But darkly from the past arose

The shifting scenes that hourly grew

More madly wild, confused, and blurr'd

Where, in the horrors of the time,

Had passed away the hope sublime

Of Israel, and the awful word

At first low mutter'd, rose on high
And spread abroad, and gathered strength
Till nothing could be heard at length
But the loud clamour, *Crucify!*

Beyond the peaceful eventide,
Amid the pelting of that storm
They still in spirit saw the form—
The sacred form of Him who died. ,
Then one disciple spake his mind:
" Ah, how we deemed this might be He
" To set our waiting Israel free:
" He raised the dead, and to the blind
" Gave back the beauty of the earth,
" The lame restored, unstopp'd deaf ears:
" He wiped away the mourners' tears,
" And in the desert none had dearth.
" Such wondrous power He seemed to wield!
" And yet we saw Him doomed to death:
" We saw Him yield His final breath—
" No soldier dead upon the field,
" But basely on the shameful Cross.

"Well we who owned Him as our Chief,

"And witnessed His majestic grief,

"Now know the greatness of our loss.

"And yet this morn all hearts were stirr'd

"To hear His sleeping form was gone,

"Though how or where was all unknown.

"No stranger tale was ever heard:

"The massive stone was rolled away,

"And beings of celestial grace,

"They said, were watching still the place.

"The wonder grew with growing day,

"For some of our own brethren went

"To see the tomb without its dead,

"And found it all as they had said;

"But none could tell what these things meant."

Unheeding Nature's loveliness,

And deaf to all but this one theme,

They wandered on as in a dream,

Like men whom heavy thoughts oppress.

But One drew near whose searching glance

Took in the meaning of the whole,

Who unawares upon them stole,

Like some pale figure in a trance.

And when He came, in words of flame

He scorched them with His fervent speech,

While they looked strangely, each to each :

" Are ye the slaves of common fame ?

" Do ye not know, O fools and blind

" Who ponder thus your moving tale,

" That not one prophet-word can fail,

" And all has happened as designed ? "

Not idly at the rabbis' feet

The Boy had sat with the unlearned,

And now their hearts within them burned

To hear Him all His lore repeat

Of prophecy in days of old.

How plots should gather round the King

Come for the world's delivering,

The former ages had foretold.

If He could triumph in His death,

And show Himself more truly great

By bearing all the rulers' hate,

And bless them with His dying breath,
In this His royalty was proved.
In days to come it would be seen
No earthly king had ever been
Like Him who had so greatly loved.

Still on His words entranced they hung,
And since the shades of night were nigh
They brought Him to their home hard by,
But knew not Him to whom they clung.
Nor He in coldness held aloof:
As Abram angels entertained,
So at their bidding He remained,
An honoured guest beneath their roof.
The Stranger took the bread and blessed:
And then, as if a curtain fell,
In Him they knew and loved so well,
They recognise their unknown guest.
Ah, what a beating of the heart!
We hear their lips His name repeat:
We see them starting to their feet,
And yet they only meet to part.

" What ! vanished ?   Was it all a dream ?
" What fantasy of sense is this ?
" That voice, that glance, were surely His,
" Yet how unreal all things seem ! "

So, on some lofty mountain height
Two friends may stand, till o'er them steals
Such rapture as the poet feels,
To see the valley bathed in light ;
But soon the spirit of the storm
Has spread his curtain over all :
From cavern depths the wild winds call
The mists that like a phalanx form.
The mountain scene is wrapt in night,
And, ere a mutual word is said,
The transient vision all has fled
Whose beauty was so exquisite.

Through darkling eve in vain they peer
For something that they cannot see,
And yet they dare aver that He
In very truth but now was here.

But when they rally from surprise,
The glorious certainty is theirs—
"*He lives, and still our nature wears.*"
One purpose moves them to arise
This gospel of delight to bear—
"That now they need not mourn Him dead"—
To those their friends dispirited,
Nursing the soul of their despair.

II. THE RETURN TO JERUSALEM.

Though weary now and travel-worn,
And night is trampling out the day,
Again the friends are on the way,
By high elated hope upborne.
Perhaps amid the fading light
When substance melteth into shade,
And forms most real seem to fade
To formless vagueness of the night,
In shadowy things they think they see
The vanish'd Master close at hand,

But when they pause and gazing stand,
Find nothing but vacuity.
Was ever walk at night like theirs?
In every trailing branch down-drooping
They seem to see a spirit stooping—
They seem to hear celestial airs.

Tired Nature doth forbear to rest,
The very trees seem listening,
The songsters of the wood still sing,
For hope has flutter'd every nest.

The veil of sense is grown so thin,
The captive spirit boundeth free:
Among the woods what things may be,
What glorious life may lurk within
The covert of their leafiness,
What spirits moving o'er the grass,
The friends are asking as they pass,
While through the night they eager press.

Their footsteps hardly touch the ground:
One soul at least has left its prison,
If Jesus slain is really risen:
They hear His voice in every sound.

At last the city looms on them,
And through the darkness gleam afar
The lights, like here and there a star,
From windows of Jerusalem.
Through silent streets they reach the door
Where hunted men are keeping close,
And every step that comes and goes
Is like a message sent before
To tell them something strange has chanced.
What knock is that?   The startled band
Might well have feared the law's grim hand,
And keenly at the comers glanced;
But none would know them for the men
Who wore to-day that look of care,
As now, with rapture in their air,
They cry that Christ is come again!

And still this age takes up the cry:
This faith has saved humanity:
Beyond the gulf of death we see
A glorious Christ enthroned on high.

Easter Day.

1.

HE is risen that was dead:
    Death shall claim Him nevermore.
He is risen, as He said,
Raptly looking on before.
Yea, they slew Him, but in vain
Set their watch, and sealed the stone.
He alone of all the slain
Death and Life has truly known.

2.

He has cast aside the coil
Of this mortal that He wore.
Crown'd fruition after toil,
Joy for tribulation sore—
This is what the Lord hath won,

Won through shame and agony :
This is what His foes have done—
" He is risen—*Come and see !*"

3.

See, the stone is rolled away !
See, the grave-clothes cast aside !
There, before the dawn, He lay,
But He could not there abide.
Now the bondage of the slave
Gone for ever, all are free :
If we doubt, that empty grave
Tells us none is Lord but He.

4.

When they struck the mortal blow,
Then the faint and failing breath
Growing momently more slow,
Seemed consummated in death :
But the Life is manifest
Over which He cast a veil,
And His promise for the rest,
We believe, can never fail.

5.

Many dying agonies
In the years to come may be,
But the ear, above the sighs,
Hears the heavenly symphony.
Death itself will breathe its last,
Shades of night will cease to fall:
Gloom and sorrow overpast,
Life will mantle upon all.

Sonnets.

ITALY.

 ITALY, whom long intestine feud
  Left torn and bleeding, though the thought
    divine
Of Freedom still imperishably thine
Never forsook thee, thou hast crushed the brood
Of evil passions warring with the good
In factious plottings. Thy unbroken line
Grew strong through brotherhood, whose touch be-
    nign
Brake off from thee the bonds of servitude.
The day is won, and the admiring world
That saw the banner of thy cause unfurled,
To droop no more till shouts of victory
Had filled the air, makes common cause with thee.
Now thou canst smile, thinking of lips that curled
At that old cry—*Italia shall be free !*

GEORGE ELIOT: IN MEMORIAM.

STRANGE prophetess, who now upon the heights
    Didst fearless tread with an Excelsior cry,
And now break forth with a mere woman's sigh
Over the wishes vain and broken lights
Of truth, that through the days and nights
Make up the sum of life—whilst asking " *Why ?* "
So vainly, thou didst bear thy spirit high,
As one who, though despairing, bravely fights
On to the end.   Thy cold philosophy
Is buried in thy grave, but there survive
Some tokens still, in aspirations strong,
Of faith in more than all thine eyes could see :
Some help thou gavest to the weak who strive
Against the great conspiracy of Wrong.

.

From Darkness into Light.

FOUNDED ON PASLM XXXII.

NO pause of pain, no refuge or escape
        In stately court, or camp, or festival !
His sin is ever there, a haunting shape
That will not leave the monarch's side ; and all
The melody of life has ceased for him.
By day, by night, before his staring eyes
A spectre passes, never growing dim.
In presence of the court he must disguise
His real infamy.   The men are few
Who know him as he is, his kingliness
Had so bewitched them, and they have no clue
To thread the subtle maze of his distress,
Or pierce the falsehood of his mimic joy.
So, hour by hour, the weary-hearted man,

O'ersated with the luxuries that cloy
The sense, sees ever where his sin began,
And how it grew, and in its mastery
O'erthrew his honour, and from the abyss
Bade visions rise no eyes but his could see.
To this has come his transient dream of bliss!

He wore a fair outside: the inward stings
Were unsuspected by the multitude.
About the court there might be mutterings
Of dark suspicion, hardly understood:
The lips of scandal here and there might hiss
Their ill surmise; but who could look on him
So self-contained, and dream of aught amiss?
He stood so high, it seemed no breath could dim
The bright effulgence of his great renown.
The " Light of Israel"—the nation's pride
Grew in the splendour of King David's crown :
None shrank, as men dishonoured, from his side.

Through all the duties of his state by day
He keeps his place, and, every inch a king,

No coward glance or gesture shall betray
The startled conscience, scared by that dread thing
That will not leave him.   But the dreary round
Has not a soul within it, and the zest
That once in rule his high-strung nature found,
He feels not now; and, though he wears his crest
As one whose pride disdains to flinch from pain,
There is a raging fire that burns within.
His lips are parched :   there is a cruel strain
Upon the mind thus haunted by its sin.

The deed is done : his dole he needs must dree.
He wanders listlessly amid the rout
Of pleasure-seekers, looking on their glee;
And yet it is as when the summer's drought
That sucks the moisture from the thirsty plain
Has turned its verdure to a dreary waste.
The mimes and minstrels ply their arts in vain
On one so sick that he has lost his taste
For all the pleasant things. The song, the dance
With which the court would chase away his gloom,

Have lost their charm ; harsh notes of dissonance
Jar on the sense, and vibrate through the room.

His gaiety was forced ; his troops of friends
Who thought they knew him, saw him wear a mask;
But when the halls are still, and Night descends,
What power shall nerve his spirit for the task
That then awaits him, when the still small voice
He needs must hear, recalls the shameful past ?
The palace gates are closed, and yet a noise
Is in his ears, and Night has power to cast
Upon the spirit such a weight of fear
That common things are draped in mystery.
For slumber will not come, and through the drear
Long hours, the visions that he may not flee
Come crowding, and his peace of heart is gone.
His life is full of broken harmonies—
What boots it now the honours he has won,
Since all the pride of life has shrunk to this ?

His sin he loves not, but it is his own,
Part of himself : he cannot sever now

His life from it.   Though sacrifice atone,
No bitterness of heart in him, no vow
Late utter'd, or his agony of tears,
Can make the thing be other than it is.
He sinn'd with others, but his spirit hears
A voice proclaiming that the sin was his.
He cannot dam the stream he caused to flow :
He has no royalty to say : " Thus far,
" O hated human sin, thy tide shall go! "
Too late !   He cannot make it cease to mar
Those other lives.   Fell, fateful though it seem,
It still must flow, and those he loved the best
Be swept, he knows not whither, on its stream.
And he is their undoer !   Love unblest
Is always cruel : only for the worse
It changeth those it claimeth for his own :
Its fatal tenderness has proved a curse,
And into gall has all its sweetness grown.

This trembling sinner, could he be the same
Whom all upheld as what a man should be,
And, seeing him so great, adored the name

Of that supreme, celestial Purity
That could so beautify a human life?
This bard and prophet, warrior and king,
Who never fainted in the hurtling strife,
Who swept his harp, and made the valleys ring
With purest melody—ah, how had he
Unloosed the bands of faith, in living men!
How had he sullied with his infamy
The purity of God! And if again
The thoughts within him would not be restrained—
The better, purer thoughts that honour good—
How would his prophet-message be disdained,
And all the sons of Belial, with their brood,
From him take fresh occasion to blaspheme!
And men would ask if any man is true,
If saintliness is nothing but a dream,
Or something worn to hide the deeds men do.

The glowing Fancy that in happier days
Soared in its flight beyond the awful sky
To look on Him whom suns and planets praise,
Or stoop'd again from aspiration high

To hill and stream, and valleys thick with corn,
Has now grown vengeful. That despairing cry
Comes from a soul in pain, whom care has worn
And wasted, till the sympathetic frame
Is implicated in its suffering.
The thronging images of sin and shame
Have ta'en such hold, and now so closely cling
It seems as if to this one use were turned
The rich endowments of the man. The thought
That in its high ecstatic mood had burned
And glowed like fire, exists to him for nought
But to construct, as by a dread machine,
An armoury of horror and dismay.

The thing he is, and all he once had been—
His purer self for ever passed away—
The early years of promise, and his fall—
His shepherd life, his youthful innocence,
The solemn rapture of the kingly call,
And then the yielding of the soul to sense,—
The calculated method of his sin,—
The formal rites, the soulless sacrifice

By which he mock'd his God, and sought to win
Before the crowd, some honour in their eyes,—
The hot fierce fire of passion now burnt out,
And yet his sin for ever by his side,—
His leaping pulse, his moisture turned to drought,
His peace of conscience broken, and his pride
Prone in the dust! surely the hand of God
Is heavy on him, and the minister
Of chastisement requires no other rod
Than that Imagination, that could stir
Those gloomy depths, and cast a lurid light
On dark recesses in the sinful soul,
Till every fancy seemed a mocking sprite,
And Thought, half dreaming, lost its self-control.
So now, in all his realm, the wretchedest
Is he whose daring feet have clomb so high
That all men bend before him, and the breast
That heaves with that untterable cry,
The breast of him who, chief and lord of all,
Could only from that majesty of height
Plunge to the depths of such an awful fall.
Thy hand is heavy on me, day and night—

So wailed the king, as, prostrate in the dark,
He felt the weight like lead upon his soul.
And yet his pain was as the kindling spark
Some breath of grace might fan into a flame.
The callousness, the dull cold pride, were gone:
Better the sorrow, bitterness, and shame
Than when the heart was hard and cold as stone.

The dry-eyed grief is like a brand that sears
And leaves a cruel scar; but when the eyes
Begin to overflow with healing tears,
Then new desires of tender longing rise
That soothe like balm, and, though the grief is there
And cannot be explained away, there flow
Pure streams of feeling, and the heart can bear
With less of pain, its crushing weight of woe.
Alone, or only mated with his sin,
He lived a secret life, and wildly sought
Amid the fiercely raging storm within,
Some refuge from the tyranny of thought;
The wound was angry; nothing soothed the pain:

His secret sin had blotted out the world :
He could not leave it, though it was his bane.
Impenitent, while scorn his proud lip curled
The day brought misery, the night no rest.
But when he stript him bare of all his pride,
And all the anguish of his soul confessed,
Then healing came, and peace.   The gulf so wide
Between the man and God, had vanish'd now :
The long pent stream of penitence burst forth,
The free confession, and the fervent vow.
For all the world to him was nothing worth
If in the blaze of that tremendous wrath
That is so pure, he still must stagger on
Half stupefied, whilst ever on his path
New dangers rise.   No gracious breast
On which to cast himself when hard bested—
No heart of love to feel for him—no zest
Of joy in life to lay that ghostly dread !
But when there passed this vision of dismay,
Into the light the lonely spirit came.
The lips that had been sealed at last could pray,
And, pouring out the story of his shame,

He felt, although he saw not, that a Hand
In blessing on his humbled head was laid,
And He to whom he came had loosed the band—
The iron band his wilful self had made.
New trust has vanquish'd now the old despair:
The exile feeling gone, once more the son
Lays bare his heart, and, through the gate of prayer,
Sees, though the past can never be undone,
How love in God can put his sin away,
And bury it in depths of that great sea
Of His forgiveness, where the light of day
Shall never find it. Now the will, made free,
Bounds with new life, and all the world is changed.
Work, worship, pleasure, all baptized anew,
Life grows harmonious. That which had deranged
Its order, until wild confusion grew,
Gone, like some nightmare whose fantastic fear
Had made the dreamer gasp beneath its weight,
The heart is glad, despite that starting tear.
Never does heart of man so palpitate
With its exceeding joy, as when the soul
That shrank in terror from the searching eye

Of God, is comforted, and now made whole,
Reknits its union with the life on high.

No penitent has ever passed in vain
Through such an agony. The heavy cloud
Has burst at last in drops of gracious rain
That leave him soften'd, chasten'd, and the proud
High spirit, broken by its inward grief,
Views with a new solemnity the scene
So many awful things have filled. Relief
Has come to him who felt the pain so keen;
Yet this is but the opening of a door
Through which there enter graces of the mind
That make him nobler. What he was before
He knew himself, was nature unrefined
By deeper travail of the soul, while yet
No peril daunted, and the pride of strength
Unbroken by the anguish of regret,
No true humility was born. At length,
The vaulting high ambition overthrown
That aimed at empire over earthly good,
There comes into his life a sweeter tone

Than in the warlike days of old, when rude
Rough soldier duties coarsened and defiled.
The heavy sigh that breaks from him betrays
A spirit solemnised, and, in the mild
Sad look that steals into the deep-lined face
Another temper shows.   As one newborn,
The life he has to live begins again.
The soul by such an inward tempest torn
Looks through the eyes, and, in the crush of men,
New power has come to him to rule the will
And exercise a mastery of sway,
To hold in check the rising growth of ill
And let the better, purer life, have play.
He who had grown so like to them in all
That dragg'd them in the dust, the better knows
Their maze of feeling, and can break the thrall
That holds them, till upon the spirit flows
True calm of feeling after much unrest.
The pride that he has laid for ever down
Was impotent for this his high behest:
But now the thorns that wreathe his kingly crown
Denote for him a greater ministry

That reaches only to its proper height
When eyes which God hath cleansed get power to see
That he is king of men, who rules by **Right**.

It needed One of yet diviner mould
To win this knowledge by the way of pain,
To see the horror, and to feel the cold
And deadly shiver, yet without a stain.
But even He must pass within the sphere
Where Evil tempts, and learn through suffering
To understand, and pity, and draw near
To all who live, and prove Himself their king.

" In all things made like unto us."

1.

CROSSBEARERS of earth, unto Thee may we turn
    Who knowest our nature ?   Thy faith did not fail
When tempted as we, though the trial was stern:
The Cross is so heavy—the bearers are frail !
The infinite pathos of many a scene
Where still they toil on with the tears in their eyes,
Thou seest and knowest: the great and the mean
In the life that is ours Thou wilt not despise.

2.

Canst Thou feel for us, Saviour, lifted so high ?
Our hunger, our thirst, our unrest Thou didst know,
And pain with its sad inarticulate cry—
All strife of the spirit, all natural woe,
Those inner mysterious pangs of the heart

Which agonise keenly the life of the good
When love seems to falter, and friendships depart,
And men by the nearest are least understood.

3.

One other thing yet—when last words are spoken,
When voices the dearest have said their farewell,
When dreams of delight lie shatter'd and broken,
And none his unutter'd emotion can tell,
Not this to Thee, Son of a woman, is strange.
The record remains—Thou hast groanéd and wept;
In the heart of the Love that knoweth no change
This grief of bereavement is treasured and kept.

4.

Thou knowest the sickness and faintness of soul
When Evil breathes on us its poisonous breath,
The tumult of feeling how hard to control,
How, like to a soul that is sick unto death,
All tempted ones are, though through grace they may
    stand;
For into the gulf of despair Thou didst look,

R 2

On its verge holding fast by faith to His Hand
Invoking Whose name Thou didst Satan rebuke.

5.

O Thou to Whom, spent with Thy conflict, there came
The tender and succouring angels of God,
When nothing we see but the terror and shame,
And sense is appall'd at the vengeance abroad—
Not with hatred or scorn, but pity divine,
Yet humanly tender, as fearing to scare,
Thou wilt look down and say—"This sorrow is Mine,
With you, My belovéd, this burden I share."

6.

We will not be fearful; oh, strengthen our will,
And warm with the breath of Thy love our desire:
Yea, teach us in darkness to trust and be still.
Not serving Our Lord for the sake of the hire,
Or for self under cover of zeal for a cause,
May we follow where Thou hast shown us the way:
If peril be round us, and fear give us pause,
The panic of sense with Thy presence allay.

To wrestle with evil, to strive for the good,
While nature protested—to Thee it belonged
To show before all men a manhood that could
Live purely, divinely, blessing when wronged.
In weakness revealing the source of our strength,
The might of Thy pureness will come to our aid:
No peril, no toil of the way, or its length
Will shame our devotion, or make us afraid.

Lament on the Death of Garfield.

1.

EVIL lords it o'er the world :
　　Cruel murder stalks abroad :
Rulers from their place are hurled :
　　Blood is streaming on the sod.

2.

Sweep the thunderbolts of wrath,
　　While the peoples stand in awe :
Speedeth vengeance on the path,
　　Scorning all established law.

3.

To the Judge of all, the cry
　　Goeth, but the air is still :
Is there None to help on high,
　　None to chain the hands of ill ?

4.

Is He but as gods that sleep
 While such deeds as these are done ?
Hath He none the ward to keep
 In the realm beyond the Sun ?

5.

Yea, He heareth: trampling feet
 Deafen not the Judge's ear:
Throned in justice is His seat,
 And the vengeance draweth near.

6.

Through these very deeds of wrong
 Stirs He deep the world's great heart:
Though the good may suffer long,
 He will come and take their part.

7.

When the kingdoms all are shaken,
 When the stars of Heaven fall,
When the good seem God-forsaken,
 By the wicked held in thrall,

8.

Us a prophet-voice has told
  Then to lift the drooping head :
Faith shall make the feeble bold,
  As they listen for His tread.

9.

Coming in a cloud with power
  We shall see the Son of Man
Glorious in His chosen hour :
  He will judge our cause who can.

10.

Nations heaving with distress,
  Voices as of storms at sea,
Vocal things, and dumb no less,
  Tell of sore perplexity.

11.

But the Righteous One has ways
  That are out of human sight :
He can thread the tangled maze
  That confuses wrong with right.

12.

Deeper, stronger love of good
Seizing on the hearts of men,
Though a brother dies, his blood
Calleth from the ground again.

13.

Yet more fervent and more strong
Virtue rises from the grave,
And immortal honours throng
Round the relics of the brave.

14.

In the soil a nation's tears
Moisten with their gracious rain,
Grow and flourish through the years
Graces sanctified by pain.

15.

Not in vain the leader dies,
Standing stedfast at his post:
Owned on high the sacrifice,
Not one drop of blood is lost.

16.

O'er the martyr sound no knell,
   Though the world must mourn for him :
Say ye only, where he fell,
   A believing requiem.

Finis.

UPON a narrow stage
   Man plays his part and frets his hour:
In youth or feeble age
   Some cord of life through loss of power
Has snapt, and all is o'er.
   The curtain falls, the actor goes,
And human eyes no more
   Shall see him save in deep repose.
But that is not the whole:
   He has but shaken off the coil
That was about his soul
   And made his life a constant toil.
It grows so wondrous clear
   That though the earthly work seemed done
The true life is not here.
   All they that dwell beneath the sun

When they have said Good-night
　To aims and strivings incomplete
Where none discerned aright
　What things were bitter, what were sweet,
Escaping from the strife,
　Can see through all the restless past
A meaning in their life,
　From which the clouds are gone at last.
For One behind the veil
　Is waiting to receive His own:
Though other helpers fail
　For their defect can He atone.
He only holds the key
　Of mysteries that daunt our faith,
And most, the mystery
　That gathers round the gate of death.
The Christian passing bell
　Proclaiming one more gone to rest,
Says softly—"All is well!"
　No evil dreams that sleep infest.

Australian Scenes.

THE EXILE.

THOUGH long ago he said farewell
    To pleasures of the seagirt strand,
To shaggy height and wooded dell,
Yet ever to the Fatherland
His spirit turns as to its home :
His heart's affections linger there.
At eve, as under some great dome
When solemn music fills the air
Proclaiming that life fleeteth fast,
There wake the sleeping memories
Of scenes and pleasures in the past,
And happy youth that once was his.
The common sounds of toil and strife
Pass from his soul in that calm hour,

And all the springtime of his life
Comes back and seems to burst in flower.

Again he is an ardent boy :
Again he hears the old Church bell
Ring out its stirring peal of joy,
Or toll its solemn last farewell.
The village green appears again
With forms that long have ceased to be :
He hears the shouts of stalwart men,
And sees the children's mimic glee,
The rustics dancing on the sward,
The wrestling bout, the fleet foot-race.
The rivals waiting the award,
And then the victor's smiling face.
Once more he wanders in the lane
Beneath the closely-whisp'ring leaves
Still pearly with the summer rain,
Or underneath the cottage eaves
He sees the graceful creepers twine
In gay festoons of leaf and flower—
The rose-spray and the eglantine

That make each lowly hut a bower.

The witching hour comes back to him

When day's expiring hectic fades,

When outlines of the trees grow dim,

And through the slowly dark'ning glades

The beauty of the evening haze

That rises, spreading like a veil,

For slumber of the night arrays

Tired Nature, when her strength doth fail.

There, where the interlacing boughs

Seem to be drawn in close embrace,

Perchance were spoken tender vows.

There looks from out the old, a face

That once had magic in its glance,

And never to the soul grows old.

He fondles still that old romance

Of early love, so often told.

Perhaps it was a dream that passed,

Yet left him better than before.

That image on his pathway cast

To Fancy opens wide the door

Through which the man he was is seen,
And all in which his life had part,
When every youthful sense was keen,
And there were beating at his heart
Conflicting feelings of delight—
Hope, love, and pride—yet, half afraid,
His young emotion shrank from sight,
And left its deepest things unsaid.

Perhaps in some now distant hour
He felt the nobler rapture glow
Through which, as by a mystic power,
Unseen, unheard, as soft winds blow,
The life divine is born within.
He heard the still but searching Voice,
Above the world's confusing din,
Above the babble, and the noise
Of yonder careless multitude.
He felt the inspiration strong,
The thirst for God, the love of good,
The great desire to vanquish wrong,
And all that makes our love divine.

Ah, life has no such hour as this
When Heaven draws near us, to refine
Our vague ideal dreams of bliss.
Did that too pass?   Did all this glow
By slow degrees die down in night?
Did vulgar poor ambitious grow?
And, by gradations all so slight
That none could trace them, did he change
Till, sinking from his first estate,
His manhood's thought took lower range?
The dream of being some one great—
The king of men whom he disdained—
Did that take fatal hold of him?
But now a purer height is gained
From which he sees the gauds are dim
That lured him on.   The early days
Declared what all his life might be,
And he has wasted on the chase
Of emptiness and vanity
The days he might have traded o'er
For God and man. Swift-footed days—

They fled, and they will come no more.
And so the worldly dream decays!

Decay most blessèd, if the Thought
That shapes a human destiny
Has come to plead with him, and taught
His disenchanted soul to see
The things that are of highest worth.
Again ascends his pure desire
Like holy incense from the earth.
As once, from God's own altar-fire
There came a messenger to touch
The sin-stained lips of one sad seer
Whose sin oppress'd his soul so much
That high desire was quenched in fear,
It well may be when eventide
Has soothed to rest the thoughts of care,
Some angel summoned to his side
May whisper to his soul, to bear
Such witness of the higher things
That all the meaning of his life
Grows clear.   He hears no angel wings.

But now the weary soulless strife
That spent and tired him so in vain
He looks upon with other eyes :
Too short the time that may remain
To seek and win a nobler prize.

The evening sky is beautiful,
And beautiful the silver haze
That rises from the vale, to cool
The fever'd heat of summer days ;
But most of all the time is sweet
Because the soul is sensitive ;
For then long-parted spirits meet
And tenderly their greetings give.
At such a time, when far from home,
Beneath some arching roof of trees
The spirit of a man may roam
In fields whose golden light he sees
With other eyes than those of sense.
The past brings back some pure regret,
And faith forecasts the evidence
Of things that are not seen as yet.

As when adown the hill there came
The tabrets of the prophet band
To put the earthly heart to shame,
This exile in a foreign land
Hears soft appealing voices come
That find him in his secret heart,
And make him feel how far from home
His life hath been.   The busy mart,
The farm, the money-changer's seat,
The mining venture, and the gold
Dug from the rocks beneath his feet—
Though these should lead to wealth untold,
The soul finds Home in none of these.
They have no sweetness: they allay
No thirst immortal: if they please,
They do but on the surface play
Of life, that craves some deeper joy.
They reach no deep, atone no sin,
And give no answer to the cry
That rises from the depths within.
As ever on the restless sea
The waves roll on their crests of foam,

In toil of gain no rest can be
To him whose spirit longs for home.

'Tis ill to leave our native Isle,
Nor tread again its mossy sod,
And yet there is a worse exile,
The exile of the soul from God.
But he who wanders far astray,
If haply on his soul should rise
The wish once more to find his way
Within the light of loving eyes,
'Tis well to know a Home there is
Where he is longed for wearily—
A better, dearer Home than this,
With room for even such as he.
However late, it waiteth still:
The soul returns unto its rest:
The Love no wanderings could chill
Receives and folds him to its breast.
No grudging elder brother's voice
Will damp the joy of the return,
But there will all the blest rejoice
That one more soul has found its bourne.

Australian Sonnets.

AN AUSTRALIAN DROUGHT.

THE sun's hot breath has stricken faint and still
    All living things: the end has come at last
Of many sanguine hopes.   The furnace blast
Across the burning desert swept to kill :
The dreams of industry are overcast
With one great terror.   All is parched, and fast
The sheep on meadows once so richly grassed
That cropt the herbage at their wanton will
Are perishing.   The river-beds are dry :
All faces gather blackness as they look
Each in the other.   Not the faintest cloud
Shows on the gleaming archway of the sky :
Men babble in their dreams of rill and brook,
And low the loftiness of man is bowed.

THE FOUNDATION OF A CHURCH.

(St. Columba's, S.A.)

WE know, O living God, Thou canst not dwell
    In temples made with hands, since boundless space
Is all too little for Thy dwelling-place ;
Yet Thou dost list to hear Thy children tell,
When thoughts too big for speech within them swell,
Of all their longings for Thy lost embrace.
Although they cannot look upon Thy face,
In Christ Thy mirror yet they know Thee well.
The walls we build will crumble and decay,
But, shelter'd in them for a little while,
The life of earth may grow to the divine,
And when the worshippers shall pass away,
Then shall they find, after the long exile,
That Thou has built for them a nobler shrine.

A VACANT SEE.

(St. Peter's Cathedral, 1882.)

THE chair is empty, and the voice unheard
    Of him who welcomed, year by year, the flock

That now have come to pray, since who shall knock
To him the Lord will open.   All are stirr'd
With strange emotion, as they see the blurr'd
Uncertain lines in their own lives.   The shock
Of change has come, and Memory has woke
The echoes from the past, of deed and word
That never more shall be again.   There rise
Regretful thoughts of years that might have been
More truly kindred with the life above.
They are abashed to think of purer eyes
Looking upon this brief and shifting scene
From yonder radiant height where all is Love.

"THE OLD ORDER CHANGETH."

"HE must increase"—so spake the Nazarite—
    "And I grow less and less."   Men living still
Catch up his words, when eyes that once were bright
Grow dim with age, and evening's mellowed light
Falls on the scene.   For the victorious will
Feels creeping on the sense a deadly chill,

And, though the mind feels all its old delight
In scenes and labours that were dear, the thrill
With which the sense responds, is growing faint.
Life has but little left for him to do
Who on the field of action was so strong:
Yet not for him the voice of weak complaint—
When old men fail, the young their work renew:
Time fleets apace, but Faith, like Art, is long.

A FAREWELL.

(NOVEMBER, 1882.)

FAREWELL, dear Home, within whose terraced shade
    The world seemed far away, and when the night
Came with its train of stars, from yonder height
The silver moonlight streaming round us played,
Although we leave thee, yet there cannot fade
The things that have been—words and tones so slight
We hardly noted them, till in the flight
Of time, the end has come: yet not the end,
For other scenes have other things in store.

Wherever human love finds room to grow,
That place is Home: may there on ours descend
Such homelike blessings as we knew of yore—
No better thing than this could Heaven bestow.

Appendices.

A.

VOICES OF DOUBT.

" The moral meaning of the whole."

" Whatever be the conquests of physical science in detail," says Canon Liddon ; " whatever amount of light it may pour on the working " and structure of the material world, all this does not dispose of the " serious question—How and why did this vast system of being come to " be ? Science may unveil in nature regular modes of working, and " name them laws ; she may show that effects supposed to be due to " some immediate interference from above are traceable to ascertained " agencies below ; she may substitute, and to a degree beyond present " anticipation, some doctrine of gradually developed life for the older " belief in permanent distinctions between living species. But the " great question still awaits her. Who furnished the original material " for the presumed development ? Who gave it the first impact ? Who " has conducted it through the successive stages of its history ? "

—*University Sermons, pp.* 40, 41.

B.

VOICES OF DOUBT.

" They enter not the Temple gate."

The same distinction between intellectual error and moral unbelief was set forth by the present author in a paper read before the Melbourne

Church Congress, from which he may be permitted for once to quote: "The thing which in Scripture is rebuked with such deep solemnity "of condemnation is not merely the intellectual error which arises from "some defective use of the reasoning faculty. It is a wrong condition "of the moral nature. which leads to a rejection of the truth, not on "account of defect in the evidence, but because of the good in it from "which the sinful nature turns with repugnance. If, then, I speak of "such a man—to take one example—as John Stuart Mill—as an "unbeliever. I use the word in its general and not in its specific sense. "I see that he rejected Christianity because he was not intellectually "satisfied with the evidence ; but when I see in him, at the same time, "the presence of Christian virtues, the purity of feeling. the sense of "justice, the reverence of heart, the subjection of self to the highest "interest of man, which are among the best results of Christianity, I "see one who in spite of his intellectual denials, did in his moral "nature fall under the spell of the truth which he fell short of believing; "and I am compelled to distinguish between the ratiocination which "fails through an exaggeration of the value of the purely logical or "the purely scientific test of truth, and that moral condition of "unbelief which is damnable because it indicates a mind depraved or "morally perverted. . . There is a witness of the Son of God in the "heart, and to that witness the moral nature in some cases responds "even where the intellect continues to be hopelessly perplexed. And "where the affections and the will are thus under the sway of a holy "influence, the best part of the man's nature has obviously yielded."— —*Record of Melbourne Church Congress*, pp. 57, 58.

C.

The piece called " A Nightfall" was written after a very peculiar Australian sunset, which vividly recalled a passage in Mr. Haweis's Music and Morals, portions of which were unconsciously inwoven. It

occurs at the close of his highly poetic analysis of Mendelssohn's
Elijah (page 361)—"At the close of some refulgent summer day, when
"the sun has set, darkness does not immediately take possession of the
"earth—the sky still pulses with pale light, and long crimson streaks
"incarnadine the west. There, as we watch, the colours change and
"flicker, thin spikes of almost impalpable radiance shoot upwards
"through the afterglow, and with celestial alchemy turn many a grey
"cloud to gold. The rising mists are caught and melted capriciously
"into violet and ruby flame—and as the eye, still dazzled with the sun,
"traverses the deserted heavens, the prospect is no doubt more peace-
"ful than when the fiery globe was there—more peaceful, for the cold
"twilight grows apace, and the eye is gradually cooled as it gazes upon
"the fading fires, until at last the subtle essences of the night have
"toned all down into a monotint of grey and passionless repose."

--- ---

D.

THE PROPHET VOICES.

" And makes the wicked hymn His praise!"

"For myself I can say that no thought has been so reassuring to
"me, when oppressed by the sight of what has seemed to me a great
"moral retrogradation, as that beautiful analogy drawn by Hartley
"between the movements of the planets as seen respectively from the
"Earth and the Sun, and the phenomena of the moral world as seen
"respectively from our own standpoint and as they would be seen from
"the centre of the whole system. For, as the occasional retrograde
"motions of the planets seen from the Earth would be all seen from
"the Sun as continuous onward circuits, so (says Hartley) if we could
"only take our stand in the Divine Benevolence, and could view all
"moral retrogradations (as we deem them) from that centre, we should

" see them as real progressions. That He 'maketh the wrath of man
"to praise Him,' or, in other words, that He turneth even the evil
" passions of men into instruments for bringing about His beneficent
" ends—has thus impressed itself on my mind as one of the most
" sublime of the utterances of that old Hebrew Poet whose profound
" religious instinct enabled him to discern what the philosophic historian
" now deduces from the experience of the past as one of its highest
" teachings."—*Dr. W. B. Carpenter on Mind and Will in Nature.*

www.ingramcontent.com/pod-product-compliance
Lightning Source LLC
Chambersburg PA
CBHW020852020726
47497CB00005B/1373